W9-BXN-288

-Book Two-

MIDNIGHT REYNOLDS

AND THE AGENCY OF SPECTRAL PROTECTION

Peachtree

CATHERINE HOLT

ALBERT WHITMAN AND COMPANY
CHICAGO, ILLINOIS

Library of Congress Cataloging-in-Publication
data is on file with the publisher.

Text copyright © 2018 by Catherine Holt
Hardcover edition first published in the United States of America in 2018
by Albert Whitman & Company
ISBN 978-0-8075-5128-8

Printed in the United States of America
10 9 8 7 6 5 4 3 2 1 BP 22 21 20 19 18

Cover art copyright © 2018 by Ayesha Lopez

For more information about Albert Whitman & Company,
visit our website at www.albertwhitman.com.

To Pam—this one is for you!

CHAPTER ONE

Midnight Reynolds tightened her grip on the stall door in the museum's restroom. Since she'd moved to the town of Berry, West Virginia, she'd stopped a one-hundred-and-fifty-year-old woman from stealing the souls of the dead, she'd made enemies with two of the most popular girls in school, *and* she'd dressed up as a Viking for Thanksgiving. But what she was about to do was more terrifying than all of those things combined.

In fact, triple it, and it still wouldn't be close.

"Come on," her best friend, Tabitha, said in an encouraging voice from the other side of the door. "It's going to be okay."

"But what if it's not?" Midnight made no effort to turn the handle. Fear leached into her bones. She'd actually been looking forward to the museum field trip until Mrs. Peyton had announced that Midnight would be paired with Logan Johnson—her crush. Which was why she was now locked in the toilet stall. "It's all been a big mistake. I'm not remotely ready. I should've known."

"If you don't come out, I'll have to climb over the stall door, and you know much I detest exercise." Tabitha's voice was mournful. "Not that I understand why it's a problem. You talk to Logan all the time. He sits our table. *He laughs at your jokes.*"

"It's complicated." Midnight reluctantly stepped out into the brightly lit restroom and sighed.

It had been six months since she'd turned twelve and discovered her special ability to see spectral energy—the souls of people who had died. All because she'd been born at midnight on Halloween (hence her weird name). And, after a small hiccup, where she'd accidentally thought spectral energy was something evil that needed to be captured, she and Tabitha had spent the last two months working for a secret organization called ASP—Agency of Spectral Protection.

Working for ASP let her combine her love of spreadsheets and time management. Plus, each week, money was transferred into her bank account to cover her expenses, with some left over for a college fund. Her boss, Peter Gallagher, had even arranged for her to have a pretend babysitting job as a cover for why she was out so much. And her work with ASP let her make up for the damage she'd done when she'd been trying to fight spectral energy.

Unfortunately, none of it helped her speak to boys. Or, in this case, *one* boy.

Nor had it changed the fact that with her mousy brown hair, large glasses, and sludge-green eyes, she looked more like a goblin than a superhero. At least, she thought so.

"After everything you've faced lately, how can you be scared of this?" Tabitha's blue eyes filled with the confusion. As usual, she was wearing all black, right down to her lipstick, which meant that her confused expression looked similar to her scornful one, but Midnight had learned to tell the difference.

Midnight fumbled around in her pocket for her spreadsheet.

"It's scary because it's messing with my system. See, here in red is school time. That's when I can just be 'regular Midnight' and have normal conversations with kids at school. Kids like Logan. And this orange is home time. It's where I'm 'family Midnight'—the obliging daughter who doesn't throw a tantrum just because she has to dress as a shield maiden for her mom's wedding, even though it's the Most Ridiculous Thing in the World. Of course Taylor's pretending to love the idea, because that's just what she does—"

"I think 'family Midnight' is getting off target." Tabitha coughed. "And I still don't see what all this has to do with today."

"Because this pink section is where I'm 'protector Midnight,' and you can clearly see the museum falls into the pink section. We came here three times last month to do research. Spending unscheduled time with Logan will make me cross pink and red. Anything could happen."

Tabitha blinked and handed back the spreadsheet. "Okay, first, you know I don't like pink. I wish you'd stop using it. And second, while I think your spreadsheets are awesome, you can't compartmentalize your life. Logan's your friend. Your good friend."

Midnight frowned. She'd come up with her spreadsheet system after reading the Agency of Spectral Protection's handbook. The handbook was split into twelve chapters, all going into great detail about how spectral protectors needed to behave in public and what they could and couldn't do.

And the most important rule of all? It was on page two:

Don't let civilians find out about spectral energy, because it could cause unnecessary attention and prevent ASP from doing our job. And when we don't do our job properly? Chaos follows.

Chaos? Not on her watch.

"But what if I slip up and talk about work? I haven't planned anything to say to him. For example, all those jokes he laughs at? You don't think I just leave them to chance, do you?" Midnight said as Tabitha dragged her out of the restroom into the foyer, where the rest of the class was milling around, taking selfies and talking in loud voices. Over to the left, their teacher, Mrs. Peyton, was deep in conversation with the museum staff.

The Berry Early History Museum was a two-story building that had thick interior columns, whose sole purpose seemed to be to make the place look spooky—at least to most kids. In the last few months, Midnight's definition of *spooky* had undergone a few changes.

"You'll be fine. If you get really stuck, you can just text me. Or you could talk about this lousy weather."

"Actually, that's not a bad idea." Midnight perked up and glanced out the window that ran down one side of the building. A gloomy, rain-soaked sky stared back at her. A true case of April showers. "My mom's been freaking out that her perfect outdoor spring wedding will be washed out. I downloaded a weather app to show her, but I think that's just made it worse."

"See, that's a start," Tabitha said as Mrs. Peyton gestured to the group.

"Okay, class. I'd like you to find your study partner," their teacher said. "You each have a sheet of questions that need to be answered, and I want you to work as a team. We'll meet back here for lunch, and then we'll go through the gold-mining exhibition."

"You can do this." Tabitha nudged Midnight toward Logan and then disappeared.

"Hey, Midnight. I wasn't sure where you were, so I grabbed an extra worksheet," Logan said with a shy smile. His thick brown hair fell in a tangle across his brow, almost covering his dark-chocolate eyes. He was wearing a green hoodie with *Elementary* written across it, with a magnifying glass next to the word. It was cute, and she knew Sherlock Holmes was his hero.

"Thanks," she gulped, not willing to admit she'd been hiding in the restroom like a coward. But Tabitha was right. Midnight had hung out with Logan plenty of times over the last couple of months, and if worst came to worst, she could always show him the weather app. It wasn't conversation gold, but it was better than reverting to the girl she once was around him. The one who couldn't even say a full sentence.

"Everyone's going to start with the geography questions, so I was thinking we should begin at the other end, with the dinosaurs. It'll be less crowded," he said, proving he was cute *and* smart.

"Good idea," Midnight said as they broke off from the rest of the class and headed to the next floor up.

"So, have you been here before?" Logan asked.

She nodded. "Yes. Tabitha and I were—" Midnight cut herself off from saying that she'd been there on ASP business. See, this was why it was a bad idea to merge sections of her spreadsheet. "Er, when we were researching...my house."

"Wow, that's cool. Did you find anything out?"

"Not much." Midnight crossed her fingers. "I guess we'll have to keep looking."

"Yeah, though imagine how freaky it would be if you found out it was haunted," he said as they reached a *Brachiosaurus* skeleton.

"Yeah, totally," Midnight agreed, not bothering to add that with all the equipment she had hidden under her bed, fixing a haunted house wouldn't be a problem.

He grinned at her, and the next forty minutes passed quickly. Apart from a couple of awkward moments, Midnight didn't say anything to embarrass herself. They gathered in the foyer where Mrs. Peyton announced that since it was still raining, they'd be eating lunch in the museum cafeteria.

Immediately, a group of kids pushed their way to the door, sending Midnight crashing into Logan. He steadied her, causing her to catch her breath.

"You think it was something we said?" His hands dropped to his side.

"That or they can smell the vegetable quiche my mom made," Midnight said as they slowly joined the line of kids heading in the same direction.

"Could be my bologna," Logan countered before suddenly taking a deep breath. "So, Midnight…I was kind of wanting to ask you something."

"About bologna?"

"No." He coughed, and his olive complexion seemed to redden. "Something else. I was thinking of going to the new Sherlock movie on Saturday."

She blinked. "Right. Well, I know you love him. I'm

sure it will be great."

"I hope so. I was wondering if you wanted to go with me."

Oh.

Oh.

Midnight blinked again. "To the movies, you mean?"

"Yeah." Logan nodded, seeming to simultaneously hold his breath. "I mean, if you want to. But if you don't, that's cool. Not everyone loves Sherlock. I get that—"

"Sure. I'll go with you," she quickly answered. Movies were like school. They were in the red column of her spreadsheet. Plenty safe.

Plus, Saturday was five days away, which meant she'd have time to prepare.

"Really?" His eyes widened and Midnight grinned, but before she could answer, Tabitha came bounding over. Her cheeks were flushed, and her scowl was nowhere to be seen.

"There you two are." Tabitha came to a halt, then looked back and forth between them, her eyes widening. "Am I interrupting something?"

"No." Logan shook his head and muttered something about having to talk to his best friend, Tyson. Without another word, he hurried away.

"What was that about?" Tabitha demanded as soon as he was gone. "Don't tell me your weird theory was true and that you accidentally told him you're a spectral protector who's saved the town on a regular basis."

Midnight shook her head, suddenly shy. "He asked me to go to the movies."

"Like a date?" Tabitha raised an eyebrow, which was her version of getting excited.

"I guess," Midnight said as they sat down and automatically swapped their lunch bags. Midnight's mom ran her own food vlog and was constantly creating new and interesting recipes. Which was great, but sometimes Midnight just wanted a peanut butter and jelly sandwich, something Tabitha was happy to provide. "Is it weird? Do you mind if I go out with him? I don't want you to feel like I'm deserting you."

Tabitha gave a dismissive snort. "Please. I'm a strong, independent woman. Okay, a strong, independent twelve-year-old. Besides, who says I don't already have plans for Saturday?"

"Really?" Midnight widened her eyes. "Like what?"

"I wasn't going to tell you until afterward, in case it was horrible. But, Tyson Carl asked me to show him around the cemetery."

Midnight's mouth opened, but she quickly closed it again. Not only was he Logan's best friend, but he was everything that Tabitha wasn't. A sports-loving, popular kid who told jokes at every opportunity. Midnight had even seen him wearing a peach-colored sweater once.

"Don't," Tabitha warned, as if reading Midnight's mind. "I'm going into it with an open mind. Okay?"

"Sure." Midnight nodded, and they spent the rest of the break discussing and comparing answers before re-joining Mrs. Peyton in the foyer. Next to her was a tall, middle-aged man with blue eyes.

"Hello, everyone. My name's Alan, and I'm the museum director," he said in a happy, singsong voice. "I hope you're all enjoying yourself. Next up, I'm going to show you our latest exhibition. It's an interactive display to let you experience the heyday of gold mining in our area. You can pan for gold, as well as see what it was like to live as a miner."

"Sounds wonderful," Mrs. Peyton said in a loud voice to cover up the groans as everyone trailed the adults through to the main wing of the museum. The lights had been dimmed (which Tabitha explained was to help preserve things), and all around were glass display cabinets. Over at the far wall, Alan pointed to a blown-up sepia-colored letter that a long-dead miner had written.

Alan directed them to the life-sized replica of a miner's cottage, with a wax miner sitting at the table. Tabitha's blue eyes gleamed as she held up her cell phone to take a photograph.

"That's Ethan Talbot," she explained to Midnight. "He was one of the first miners to actually strike it rich. He owned the Berry National Bank and is buried in that tall mausoleum with the spooky angel on top."

Of course he was.

Midnight bit back a smile. No wonder Tyson had asked her for a guided tour. When it came to the Berry Cemetery, Tabitha was an expert.

"Over to the left are several traditional quilts that have been donated by the Perkins family," Alan said. "They were made in the late 1800s, and the fabrics tell a history of the time. And finally, the pinnacle of the show. The first piece of gold that Ethan Talbot found on his claim. It's called Sweet Wednesday."

Alan pointed to a freestanding white plinth that was covered in glass. Sweet Wednesday was as big as Midnight's fist, and even with the dull lights, it glittered like a disco ball. At that moment, a security guard appeared at Alan's side and whispered something.

"Excuse me for just one moment. This won't take long," Alan said.

"Of course." Mrs. Peyton motioned for the class to gather around Sweet Wednesday as she read from the plaque. "It was discovered in a gully at the bottom of the Madison Valley and weighs two hundred and sixty-eight ounces. At one time—"

"Hey, why does it look so weird?" Reuben interjected.

"Reuben," Mrs. Peyton growled. "How many times do I have to tell you to behave? If you can't find your manners, then you can wait in the bus."

"But it *is* weird," Reuben insisted. They all watched as the large gold nugget collapsed in on itself, like ice cream melting on the pavement. Amber liquid spread out across the bottom of the display and dripped down the plinth.

Mrs. Peyton let out a surprised gasp.

"It looks like it's been hit by an invisibility ray," someone else called out as the gold continued to melt.

"No, idiot. It's not invisible. Must be a heat ray," another voice chimed.

"I can assure you there's not an invisibility ray *or* a heat ray," Mrs. Peyton retorted, though her brows were drawn together. "I'm sure there's a logical explanation. Perhaps it's part of the new interactive experience?"

"But I was on the museum website last night, and there was no mention of any melting gold. What would be the point?" Tabitha frowned and took another photo.

Alan reappeared. "Sorry about that, folks. Now, where were we?"

"Actually…" Mrs. Peyton turned to him. "We're all very curious what this is meant to be. Is it some kind of virtual reality exhibition?"

"I'm not sure I understand what you're talking about." Alan gave the teacher a blank look before turning to the plinth as Sweet Wednesday evaporated entirely from sight.

At the same time, Midnight's skin puckered, and the sound of a thousand buzzing bees echoed in her ear. Sparks of electricity cut through the air, fizzing and crackling with rage. They were followed by tendrils of dark fog, reaching through the room like fingers, and hidden to everyone but her.

It was what happened when spectral energy was trapped.

She pushed her glasses further up her nose. Once upon a time, she'd hated them, but then she'd discovered that they helped her see spectral energy, and now she always wore them.

"Something's wrong," she whispered, and Tabitha stifled a gasp.

"No. Way. Do you mean you can—"

"Yes." Midnight cut her off, just as their cell phones beeped a distinctive pattern. It was the app that always let them know when spectral energy was trapped. Midnight didn't need to look at the map to find the location. It was right there in the museum. Panic pounded in her chest, but before she could talk to Tabitha, Alan clapped his hands together, his voice high-pitched and panicked.

"Security," he shouted. "Lock down the museum. Sweet Wednesday has been stolen."

CHAPTER TWO

A siren rang out so loud that the floor vibrated, and security guards swarmed in. Somewhere a switch was pressed, and bright light flooded the room, which only seemed to increase the chaos all around them. Excited students took photos of the empty plinth as agitated mothers tried to stop small children from screaming and crying. Mrs. Peyton hurried over to one of the security guards and was soon joined by Alan.

But all Midnight cared about was the spectral energy.

On its own, spectral energy was harmless.

Just thousands of tiny rainbow-colored snowflakes that floated and danced through the air as they made their way to their final resting place, the Afterglow. The reason there was so much spectral energy in Berry was because the entire town was surrounded by a large ripple of electromagnetic current known as the Black Stream, which acted like a doorway to the Afterglow.

However, the downside of the Black Stream was that spectral energy could become trapped in inanimate objects, particularly glass, copper, and brass. When this happened, it became a dark force, known as planodiume.

And no one knew better than Midnight just how dangerous planodiume could be. It was like a disease that infected those around it with dangerous thoughts, encouraging them to commit horrific crimes. It could also be harnessed and used as a source of power or immortality.

Her old mentor-turned-nemesis, Miss Appleby, had used it for years to stop herself from aging. But in the process, it had turned her into a murderer—someone who'd happily poisoned both her husband and her step-daughter, George and Eliza Irongate. Miss Appleby had also tried to kill Midnight and Tabitha.

In other words, planodiume was bad, and it was

Midnight's job to release it before it could cause trouble.

She swallowed hard as the black fog spread across the room, weaving in and out of the oblivious crowd.

"Is it coming from where Sweet Wednesday was?" Tabitha's face tightened. Clearly, she was frustrated that she couldn't see what Midnight could.

Midnight shook her head. "No, but whatever it's trapped in, it's built up very quickly. I've never seen anything like it. The question is, do I try to release it now, or should I wait until after school when there aren't so many people around?"

People that she knew. People like Logan.

Page eight of the ASP guidebook came to mind:

> Raising civilian suspicion should be avoided at all costs. Our best work is done in the shadows, because trying to explain a phenomenon to those who can't actively see it normally backfires. (Please see chapters nine and ten for documented examples.)

"I think you should wait. For starters, we don't know if it's connected to what just happened. If it is, it could be different than everything else you've dealt with," Tabitha said, just as Mrs. Peyton gave a sharp whistle and raised her hand in the air to signal their attention. Everyone automatically lifted their own hands to show they were listening.

"Students. In order to let the police do their jobs, we need to move quickly and quietly back into the foyer. There, we will line up and walk through the X-ray scanner the security guards are setting up. This is protocol when anything has been stolen. Once that's done, we can return to school, and the police will take statements there."

Midnight froze. "Did she just say X-ray scanner?"

"Why? Don't tell me you stole something while you were here," Tabitha said.

"Not exactly," Midnight confessed as she held up her backpack. She unzipped it just enough for Tabitha to see what looked like a ray gun, nestled next to Midnight's notepad. It had a gleaming wooden handle, a thick copper barrel covered in tubes and dials, and a long nozzle with a glass canister that ran along the top.

"You brought CARA with you?" Tabitha's voice hit

a high note, and a couple of heads turned around, but Tabitha shot them her deadpan glare and they quickly turned away. "I thought we'd discussed this. No bringing weapons to school. Or the museum."

"I know." Midnight zipped up her backpack and pretended it didn't weigh a ton. The device was a carbonic resonator, used to stop spectral energy from getting trapped in inanimate objects. But "carbonic resonator" was a mouthful, so they'd quickly nicknamed it CARA. Midnight let out a miserable sigh. "If they find it on me, life as we know it will be over. I'll be the crazy girl who got caught with a weapon at the museum."

More to the point, her cover with the Agency of Spectral Protection would be totally blown. Not to mention the subclause that clearly stated:

All agency weapons must be hidden from public view.
At. All. Times.

"And if you get caught sneaking around the museum releasing spectral energy that no one but you can see, life will also be over." Tabitha's brow furrowed. "I'm starting to see why you didn't want the different parts of your life to cross over."

"This definitely wasn't on today's to-do list. I'll have to find and release the spectral energy, and then hide CARA until tomorrow." Another wave of hideous darkness crashed through the room like an incoming tide.

"As far as plans go, it's not ideal. We don't even know what we're dealing with." Tabitha's face went pale as two police officers walked into the room, bringing the chilly weather with them. Over to the left, Mrs. Peyton was still trying to round everyone up, while simultaneously answering her cell phone.

"I know." Midnight gulped. "But I can't see any other option."

"Okay." Tabitha gave a decisive nod of her head. "You'd better go while it's crazy. If Mrs. Peyton asks, I'll say you went to the restroom. And keep your cell phone nearby. I'll text Peter and tell him about the melting gold, in case he knows something."

Midnight fingers tightened around her backpack. She hunched her shoulders and casually wandered over to the drinking fountain as if getting some water, before slipping out of the room.

The museum's foyer was just as frantic as the main room. The large wooden doors were shut, and there were two officers standing guard in front of them. Thankfully, they seemed focused on keeping people from leaving and didn't pay attention to a twelve-year-old girl with a heavy backpack slipping into the cafeteria.

The cafeteria was filled with spectral energy, but there was no sign of the real source. And without the source, Midnight was powerless to stop it. She ducked behind a post as a couple of museum workers went past. Once they'd gone, she calmed herself down and tuned in to the high-pitched buzz that was still throbbing in her ears.

She followed it up to the second floor and over to a corridor with a No Admittance sign hanging on the wall. Midnight paused. She didn't want to get into trouble for sneaking into another part of the museum. But it would be worse if people were exposed to planodiume for too long. The history of the town was peppered with traumatic events that had been caused by the very same thing—from a mining explosion in the late 1800s to a fire that destroyed an orphanage, leaving forty kids dead.

Long fingers of darkness snaked around Midnight's body, hissing in her ear. She increased her pace until she reached a storeroom.

Midnight tugged at the door as spectral energy oozed out from underneath it, but the door was locked. She'd had to deal with spectral energy from behind a locked door before, but this time she didn't know what she was facing, which made it risky. Plus, she still needed to hide CARA somewhere. She hurried back down the corridor and spotted a cleaning cart filled with spray bottles and cloths.

Please let there be a key.

She tried to act casual, even though her heart was pumping. On top of the cart was a cleaning roster, some trash that had been picked up…and a swipe card. She reached out for it and darted back to the room. As she swiped the card, the lock beeped and a red light flashed.

She stepped inside. The room was about the size of her bedroom, with one small window that let her see the gloomy, rain-soaked sky.

Old museum displays were scattered haphazardly around the floor, and several potted plants lay wilted and dead. Midnight shivered. It took a lot of trapped spectral energy to kill plants. She hoped that they'd only died because someone had forgotten to water them. She scanned the room until she came to a huge gilt-framed mirror propped against the wall.

Spectral energy billowed out of it, and a putrid smell filled her nostrils.

Midnight gagged as she fumbled with her backpack to pull CARA out.

Some of her panic lessened as her fingers slid over the weapon's familiar brass trigger. The sooner she did this, the safer everyone would be.

She pressed down, and a rush of white light burst out of CARA, hurtling directly into the mirror. The mirror shook with anger, and the swirling black fog pulsed in response as a blurred face flickered on the mirror, like a trapped reflection.

Fear jabbed at her ribs, but Midnight held CARA steady.

The face disappeared, and the terrible dark energy that

had been scattered around the museum was drawn back into the room, seeping under the doorway and slithering toward the old mirror.

The energy swirled around the room like a tornado, as if trying to fight what was happening. CARA let out a final shudder as the darkness vanished, replaced by pale-pink light that flooded the room before finally disappearing from sight.

It was over—whatever it had been.

Normally when Midnight released spectral energy, it would separate and turn back into its natural snow-flake-like form. But nothing about this had been normal. From the face in the mirror to the hideous smell, or the way the dark energy had slithered back into the mirror.

Midnight's shoulders sagged as she took out the handheld device that ASP had issued her. It measured room temperature, gas buildup, and a list of other things that Midnight didn't quite understand. Thankfully, it also looked like a cell phone, which meant that if anyone found it, it wouldn't arouse suspicion.

The device whirled and lights flashed as she walked around the room as she'd been taught. A sharp beep let her know the readings were complete. She put the device away and started searching for somewhere to hide CARA—which, unfortunately, did *not* look like a cell phone.

A large trunk under the window was filled with posters from past exhibitions. Midnight laid the weapon down and then covered it up as best she could, remembering page eight of the handbook:

> Under no circumstances should equipment be left unsupervised.

She shut the trunk and pocketed the swipe card. Once she'd retrieved CARA, she'd return the card. Then she headed back downstairs and rejoined her class as they lined up in front of the X-ray machine. The good news was that there was no sign of spectral energy.

Midnight wove her way through the crowd until she reached her friend.

"How did it go?" Tabitha asked, her voice not much above a whisper. "Did you find it?"

"It was behind a locked door. I had to steal a swipe card," Midnight said as they shuffled forward.

Tabitha widened her eyes. "Wow."

"I know," Midnight said. "But it does clearly state in the handbook that sometimes the greater good outweighs smaller considerations."

"Hey, I'm not judging," Tabitha said. "So, where was it?"

"It was in a mirror in an old storeroom, which meant I could get to it without being seen. I've also hidden CARA in a trunk up there." All around her, kids were discussing what had happened, oblivious to the danger they'd just been in. Midnight's arms shook from the exertion.

"But?" Tabitha said as if sensing there was something Midnight wasn't telling her. "I take it this wasn't a textbook case."

"Not exactly. There was a face in the mirror," Midnight said. Despite what people normally thought of ghosts, the only face Midnight had ever seen was that of twelve-year-old Eliza Irongate, who had been murdered by her stepmother, Miss Appleby. And even then, Midnight had only seen it for the briefest of moments.

"What?" Tabitha squeaked. "Like a human face?"

"I think so, though it was so blurry and it happened so quickly that it was hard to tell. Plus, there was a really bad smell. Like vomit bad. Have you heard from Peter?"

"No." Tabitha shook her head as they reached the front of the line. Midnight put her backpack on the scanner and watched as it went through the X-ray. Two guards studied the monitor before nodding their heads in approval.

"Next." The guard thrust her backpack at her and gestured for Tabitha to put hers through the machine. The good news was that Midnight hadn't been caught. The bad news was that she had absolutely no idea what had caused the strange spectral energy or the creepy face in the mirror. Or, how it related to the melted gold. All she knew was that it was something bad, and that she hoped it didn't get worse before she figured out what was going on.

CHAPTER THREE

Her mom looked up from her sewing machine as Midnight walked into the kitchen. It was a big, open room with a long, scrubbed pine table that tended to be the hub of the house. Against one wall was a huge old-fashioned cabinet piled high with plates and glasses and heavy silver cutlery, while pots of herbs grew in old wooden boxes all around the room.

Midnight was pleased to finally be home. Between giving a police statement and being warned again by Mrs. Peyton not to spread the story of the disappearing nugget, it had been a long afternoon. She sat down at the table and reached for an apple.

"How was school?" her mom asked.

Let's see. A massive lump of gold melted away. I got asked on a date. Oh, and there was planodiume at the museum. Unfortunately, none of those answers would let her escape to her bedroom. All she wanted was to talk to Peter about the report she'd filed.

"It was okay." Midnight took off her glasses and rubbed her eyes.

"So, were you there when the gold disappeared?" Phil looked up from the leather breastplate he'd been polishing.

Midnight turned toward him. "How do you know about it?"

When her mom had first announced she was going to marry Phil, Midnight hadn't been very happy. All he seemed to talk about were Vikings and how to fix cars. But after he'd inadvertently helped her stop Miss Appleby (without asking any questions), she'd warmed to him. Plus, there was no doubt her mom was happier when he was around. Even if he did want to get married wearing a full Viking costume and surrounded by his fellow reenactors who went by the name Sons of a Gunnar.

"It's been all over the news." Phil put aside his polishing cloth.

"Oh," Midnight said. So much for the museum wanting to keep the story under wraps.

"Did it really just disappear?" her mom asked. Her blond hair fell in curls around her face, and her normally bright-blue eyes had shadows under them that seemed to get darker the closer the wedding date got.

"More like melted," Midnight said before relaying everything—minus the parts that involved her, of course.

"Do they have any theories about what happened?" Phil asked just as Midnight's sixteen-year-old sister, Taylor, flounced into the kitchen. Raindrops clung to the tiny denim jacket she was wearing, and when she shook her long hair, water hit Midnight in the face.

"Watch it," Midnight complained, wiping away the moisture.

"Not my fault it's raining," Taylor retorted. "And please tell me you weren't talking about that stupid piece of gold. I swear I'm going to scream if I have to listen to one more story about it."

"It's a big deal," Phil said.

"And Midnight was there when it happened," their mom added. "It's hard to believe the gold really melted."

Taylor snorted. "That's because it's a hoax. Anyone with eyes can see that. Dylan says it's all just smoke and mirrors."

At the mention of Dylan's name, Midnight silently groaned, and even her mom rolled her eyes. Taylor had been dating her new boyfriend for a month, and lately every sentence that came out of her month seemed to include the words *Dylan says*.

"Even if that's the case, how it was done is still a mystery," their mom said. "Several of the people in Midnight's class caught it on video. Plus, the police came right after, and there was no sign of what caused the gold to melt."

"Well, as fascinating as this is, I need to take a shower." Taylor gave a nonchalant shrug to suggest that they were all talking nonsense. "I'm completely drenched. This freaking weather—"

"Actually…" Phil uncharacteristically cut in. "Maggie, I got those pickled elderberries you wanted. They're in the living room next to the Mammen ax."

Mammen ax? Midnight wasn't sure she wanted to know what that was.

"Thank you, honey. I'll go get them." Her mom immediately disappeared into the other room. Phil turned to Midnight and Taylor. His brow was crinkled, and his mouth was turned down.

"I wanted to talk to you both about the weather. Your mom's starting to fret that it won't clear up before the wedding. It's a bit hard to stand on a hillside in a field of daisies and daffodils when the hill's turned to mud. So, I was thinking it might be a good idea not to mention the rain. Instead, just focus on the fact it can't keep raining forever."

"Yes, but Dylan says—" Taylor folded her arms before Midnight glared at her. "Fine. No mention of the weather."

"I won't either," Midnight promised, just as her cell phone rang with the tone she'd assigned to her boss. He lived in England but seemed to always be traveling around the world, which made it incredibly hard to get hold of him. It was also why she needed to take the call. She scrambled to her feet, mumbling something about homework, but it wasn't until she was safely in her bedroom that she dared to answer.

"Midnight, my apologies on the delay. I'm in Russia, dealing with an Afterglow fracture," Peter said matter-of-factly in his English accent, as if Midnight should know what an Afterglow fracture was. "I've just received your report and have been studying the news feeds. How unfortunate that the story's been picked up by a few national papers."

"It made the papers?" Midnight winced, thinking of page thirty-one of the manual:

> One of ASP's biggest priorities is to keep all mention of
> spectral energy out of the press. This cannot be empha-
> sized enough. Please see chapter ten for case studies.

"Can you talk me through what happened?" Peter asked.

"Of course." Midnight faithfully recounted everything, this time not leaving out the part about spectral energy, the strange face, or her own involvement. "Have you come across this before?"

"There have been rumors floating around for years about a device that draws on the Black Stream. Somehow it drags down spectral energy and turns it into a power source to attack the particles of an object, sending them to another location while simultaneously creating a replica. Unfortunately, the replicas aren't designed to last."

"Wait? So you think that Sweet Wednesday was stolen before today and that what we saw was just a replica?" Midnight sucked in a sharp breath.

"It seems the most obvious answer, and as the principle known as Occam's razor proposes, the most obvious answer is usually the right one. However, we've never had definitive proof that such a weapon exists."

"I can't believe someone would do that," Midnight said, horrified. She'd fought so hard to help spectral energy travel safely across to the Afterglow. The idea of it being dragged back to earth and turned into something dark and dangerous was depressing.

Then something else occurred to her.

"Before I stopped Miss Appleby, no one even knew that Berry *was* a Black Stream. So, does that mean this is my fault?"

"Absolutely not. Midnight, this isn't anything you have done. I'm extraordinarily proud of how hard you've been working. Truly, it's a credit. Evil people exist everywhere. Whoever this is, you didn't put the notion of thieving into their head. But we need to find out who's behind it before things get serious."

Midnight sat back down and rubbed her brow. "Serious? What will happen?"

"The more energy that's drained from the Black Stream, the more unstable the area will become. There might be small earthquakes and tremors, cyclones. Excessive rain."

"Rain?" Midnight gulped as she looked out of the window. The gray afternoon was broken only by the swaying arms of the water-sodden trees. Cars drove past, sluicing through the giant lakes that had formed on the sides of the streets. "All the rain is because of what happened at the museum?"

"It's because of what's happening to the Black Stream. And if we don't get to the source of it, things will get worse. Which is why I'm going to need your help to track down who's behind it."

"You want me to find a gold thief? I wouldn't even know where to start."

"I know it's a lot to ask, but…" His voice was grim as it trailed off. "There's something else. The reason the spectral energy you released at the museum was so intense is because the person responsible has been exposed to too much planodiume too quickly. The body gets overloaded and needs to get rid of it, like a snake sheds its skin. We call it a rupture."

"The horrible smell, the face in the mirror, and the intensity all happened because the villain drew spectral energy from the Black Stream to steal the gold?"

"Correct. And that face in the mirror would've been the person who suffered the rupture. I don't suppose you got a clear look at it?"

"No." Midnight shook her head. "It all happened so quickly."

"I understand. And I know it's a lot to ask. But I really need your help. Otherwise I'll have to pull Jimmy from the Bermuda business. Or Terrance from Loch Ness."

Midnight turned away from the window as the chaos of the day reran through her mind. It was already hard to keep things separate. Her colors were blurring.

The answer had to be no. She was twelve, and her plate was already full. There was no room in her spreadsheet for crime. Or planodiume ruptures.

But if she said yes, she could stop more spectral energy from being trapped and, at the same time, stop all the rain and give her mom the perfect wedding. Besides, she had the rules and her spreadsheets to ensure that she didn't mess it up.

"Okay, I'll investigate," Midnight said before making an excuse about dinner.

Once again, she was dealing with something dangerous.

CHAPTER FOUR

"He wants us to *what*?" Tabitha yelped the next morning as they huddled behind their devices, while their English teacher tried to stream a YouTube clip from her laptop The fact that she'd asked Brent Rider to help her meant it would take at least ten minutes.

"Find the thief, or else this rain will never stop," Midnight repeated. Not that she was surprised at Tabitha's reaction. She was still getting used to the idea herself.

"But that's crazy. Did you explain to him that we're not some stupid television show where kids solve crime in a wild and wacky way?"

"He sounded really worried and was going to send someone else to investigate."

"Better them than us." Tabitha snorted. "I mean, it's one thing to help the dead cross over. But finding a thief is just so mundane."

"Actually, I was thinking it was dangerous," Midnight said. "The person's been exposed to high levels of planodiume, and when the body tries to get rid of it, that causes ruptures. Which is why I had so much trouble releasing the spectral energy yesterday. It's like they're leaving a trail of evil behind them, and according to Peter, it will only get worse."

Like what happened with Miss Appleby.

Once upon a time, Miss Appleby been normal, but the more planodiume she used, the more evil she became. First killing her husband and stepdaughter and then trying to kill Midnight and Tabitha. The most terrifying part was that she'd had no remorse about what she'd done.

"I guess that makes it better." Tabitha's stubborn expression faded. "And I suppose it's not the first time we've searched for a mysterious weapon."

Midnight nodded.

The only way they'd been able to stop Miss Appleby had been to find a weapon that George Irongate had built way back in 1895. George had also been able to see spectral energy and he'd had invented the spectral transformer to turn the energy into a power source. Unfortunately, after he married Natasha Appleby, he discovered that spectral energy was only dangerous when it was clumped together. Feeling terrible at what he'd done, he invented a second weapon, the carbonic resonator, to reverse the damage he'd caused.

But six months ago, the ghostly form of Eliza Irongate had helped them find the weapon. This time, they were on their own.

Midnight pulled up a new spreadsheet so that they could start collecting data. "I did some research on Wikipedia last night. We need to look for someone who has motive, means, and opportunity. I have to go back to the museum to collect CARA, so I thought we could look for clues and ask around while we're there."

"Surely the police would've found everything." Tabitha didn't sound convinced.

"Yes, but they're looking for clues like fingerprints. We'll be looking for other things," Midnight said before wrinkling her nose. "Plus, Peter told me that the face I saw in the mirror belonged to the thief. I've been researching ghost photography, and we could try to take a photograph to see if it will show up."

"I suppose I could try," Tabitha said just as a familiar voice floated out from the back of the class.

Savannah Hanson.

Midnight froze. When she had first arrived in Berry, she'd been friends with Savannah and her sidekick, Lucy. Back then, all Midnight had cared about was fitting in. But she'd learned the hard way how dangerous that could be. Thankfully, these days Sav and Lucy ignored Midnight every chance they got.

"And I swear it was as if my life went flashing before my eyes," Sav said, holding court to an enraptured audience. She was wearing a white lace blouse and a pair of jeans that cost more than Midnight's allowance for the entire year, and her arm was draped dramatically across her brow.

"It was so intense." Lucy shuddered in agreement.

"Plus, Sav felt an eerie presence. Like she was being touched by the supernatural. I think she has the gift."

"I don't think I do," Sav protested as she fiddled with her golden hair. "Though my grandmother did. Plus I always seem to know when something bad's going to happen."

"Like when Lucas almost spilled soda on your favorite white shirt, but you moved just in time," Malie Wheeler said, her dark eyes intense. She'd moved from Hawaii to Berry about the same time Midnight had arrived. Recently, Sav and Lucy had adopted her, changing her anime T-shirts and jeans, and tying back her glorious dark curls into a sleek ponytail. Much like what they'd done with Midnight, who'd been fool enough to go along with it. Then Malie seemed to notice Midnight was staring at them. "What you looking at, freak?"

"Not you, that's for sure," Tabitha cut in before glancing back at Midnight. "Are you okay?"

"I'm fine. It's just weird seeing what I used to be like."

"You were never that bad," Tabitha said. "Plus, when Malie first arrived, she was always in the library researching, so Mrs. Crown introduced us, thinking we would have stuff in common. Not so much. She looked at me like I was something on the bottom of her shoe. She was destined to be friends with those two."

"Still, I feel sorry for her," Midnight said, but before Tabitha could respond, the movie came on, and their teacher called the class to attention.

* * *

"I don't think the museum has been this busy, since... well, never," Tabitha said later that afternoon as she and Tabitha climbed the steps to the redbrick building. Despite the pouring rain and the darkened skies, crowds were milling all around the building. A group of people nearby took selfies and spoke in hushed voices.

"I take it they're not all here for the new gold-mining exhibition." Midnight shut her umbrella and tried to shake the rain from her coat.

"No. It's a sad reflection on our society that more people come to the museum to see something that *isn't* there, as opposed to all the things that *are* there." Tabitha lowered her own umbrella. Her black hair fluttered in the breeze as they elbowed their way through the crowds to the entrance.

"Okay. We need to find out as much information as possible, while remembering to act natural and casual. Like it's no big deal," Midnight instructed, knowing that Tabitha's direct approach wasn't always appreciated.

"Right. Act casual. Like it's no big deal. I can do that." Tabitha marched up to the woman in the ticket booth. She handed over her yearly pass, which let her get in for free and also made Midnight's ticket cheaper.

"That will be eight dollars," the woman said as she swiped Tabitha's museum card.

"Thank you." Tabitha paid the money for Midnight's ticket, then leaned forward. "So, that was pretty crazy yesterday. Any new information on what happened?"

"Nope." The woman pointed to the notice taped to the window between them. It read: *Please direct any inquiries about yesterday's incident to the Media Department.*

"That's it? You're not even going to humor me with an update? Are you serious?" Tabitha said, two red spots forming on her cheeks.

"Do I look like I'm a fan of jesting?" the woman deadpanned. "If you want to know what happened, read the paper like everyone else."

"Oh yes, because the newspapers never lie." Tabitha's blue eyes flashed. "In research, we're always told to go to the original source, and yet you're telling me that there's *nothing* you can do to help me?" She probably would've said more, but Midnight grabbed her hand and dragged her away.

"We might need to refine our interview techniques," Midnight said as they threaded their way through to the main room where Sweet Wednesday had been. Everywhere they looked, people were taking photos and talking in scripted voices to whatever social media audience they were streaming too. The entrance fee didn't seem to be deterring the gawkers.

"Yeah, or find someone who hasn't let the power go to their heads," Tabitha muttered as she glanced around. "You know what annoys me the most? I come here all the time. You'd think it would give me some kind of inside connection. Actually, there's Wendy from the archives. She was the one who helped me find out the history of that weird stone at the top of Merrick Hill. Do you want to wait here while I go and talk to her, or should we get CARA first?"

"No, you should definitely talk to her. I'll wait upstairs."

Tabitha made her way through the crowd, her black skirt billowing around her, and Midnight climbed the stairs to the second floor. Elbows jabbed her as she squeezed her way over to where a group of museum staff was standing. Perhaps she could catch something important?

"Midnight, hey," a voice called out, and she spun in surprise to see Logan and his three-year-old sister standing in front of her. "I didn't expect to see you here."

That would make two of them. She swallowed down her panic. Talking to Logan was stressful at the best of times. Especially when she was unprepared. But while she was on a secret mission to catch a gold thief, it was even worse.

"Oh," she said, wishing she'd come up with a cover story. "Er, you know what Tabitha's like. She can't keep away from this place. I wish it wasn't so busy though."

"Tell me about it," Logan said. "Bella saw it on the news last night and insisted on coming."

"Hey, Midnight," Bella said with a toothy smile as she hung off her brother's arms like a monkey. "We're trying to find the missing gold. Do you want to help us? Though don't tell anyone because it's a secret."

"Remind me to go over what a secret means," Logan said, smiling apologetically. "And we're not really looking for it. That would be crazy, right?"

"Right." Midnight gulped as Bella tugged at Logan's arm again. "Totally crazy."

"Okay, well, we'd better get going. But I'll see you at school tomorrow," Logan said.

"Sure. Bye," Midnight said as she watched Bella drag Logan away.

Tabitha appeared at her side several seconds later. "What's he doing here?"

"Apparently, Bella wanted to see where the gold disappeared."

"Yeah, well, she's not alone. I spoke to Wendy, but all she could tell me was the museum was having its busiest day ever, and if there had been any developments on the case, the staff didn't know about it."

"I guess it was a long shot." Midnight clutched at the swipe card as they reached the area with the OFF LIMITS sign. She just hoped the card still worked.

Thanks to the throngs of people, no one noticed as they slipped past and Midnight swiped the key lock. A light flashed, and the door clicked open.

The room was just as she'd left it, though without the swirling darkness, it was bigger than she'd first realized. There was a door at the far end that she hadn't noticed before.

"I wonder if this is the way the villain came in?"

"It's possible," Tabitha said.

"This mirror gives me the creeps," Midnight said, staring at her reflection. Green eyes, straight brown hair, and a downturned mouth stared back at her. She shuddered and turned away.

"Me too." Tabitha held up her phone and took a photograph before studying the screen. "No sign of the villain's face. Just us. But I'll take some more shots that we can enlarge on the computer when we get home. Then we can search this place and leave."

"Finally, a plan that I agree with." Midnight walked over to the trunk and lifted up the old museum posters to where CARA was still nestled.

Thank goodness.

She lifted the copper and brass weapon. The glass tank that ran along the nozzle was still steamed up from when Midnight had used it, and the dials were set to red as a reminder that it needed cleaning. She mentally added that to her to-do list and carefully packed CARA away.

She was just closing the trunk when something bright caught her eye.

It was a silver button. Thread was still dangling from it, as if it had snagged on the trunk when someone raced past.

"Have you found a clue?"

"I'm not sure." Midnight tucked the button into her pocket and searched the rest of the room. Unfortunately, the other doorway just proved to be a supply closet.

They jumped at the sound of the loudspeaker, announcing that the museum would be closing in ten minutes, and decided it was time to leave. Midnight returned the swipe card at the information counter while no one was looking, and they walked outside. So far, the only thing they'd discovered was that finding the villain was going to be harder than they'd thought.

CHAPTER FIVE

"Is there something you forgot to tell me?" her mom asked on Wednesday morning as Midnight came into the kitchen. Her mom was repositioning one of the tall lights that she used when she was filming her weekly cooking vlog. The air was laden with the heady scent of curry and the sharp tang of freshly diced onion. Midnight knew that in thirty minutes, anyone who was still in the kitchen would be roped into taking part in the video.

"What are you talking about?" Midnight blinked, then spotted Tabitha sitting at the long table. Today's black ensemble included a beret and a long, black coat.

Her friend was also wearing a super-guilty expression, as she mouthed the word *sorry*.

Midnight's mind raced. Had Tabitha mentioned spectral energy? Or their new mission to hunt down thieves? Or that Midnight was secretly working for an organization in England with a list of rules as long as her arm? Or—

"About your date with Logan on Saturday," Midnight's mom clarified as she walked over to the second light and moved it to the left.

Oh. That.

Midnight glanced at Tabitha, who was studiously examining the hem of her black shirt. In front of her was a plate with some brown crumbs. Midnight groaned. Tabitha was a sucker for vegan brownies.

"Sorry. I was going to tell you, but then the whole thing with the disappearing gold nugget came up," Midnight said. Not to mention the fact she now had to find it. "Do you mind? It's the afternoon matinee, and his mom's going to take us and then drop me home," Midnight rambled. Hopefully her mom would think her blush was because of the heat of the stove.

"Of course I don't mind. I'm pleased you're going out. And Tabitha told me she's also got a date."

Midnight raised her eyebrow as she turned to Tabitha. "How long have you been here?" She made a mental note to start meeting her friend outside the house. Not that she knew why Tabitha had insisted on coming over so early. She'd sent Midnight a text last night telling her to be ready by seven thirty.

"Not long." Tabitha jumped to her feet. "Your mom gave me one of her breakfast brownies. You know what happens when I eat them."

"It's my secret weapon." Midnight's mom grinned. "Now, if you two girls are free before school, I'd love for you to be in today's video. We're making vegetable pakoras."

"Actually, we need to go to the library," Tabitha said quickly, well aware that Midnight's mom tried to rope everyone into her videos.

"Well, far be it from me to stop the pair of you from learning." Her mom gave them both a warm smile. "Hopefully it will clear this afternoon. Phil seems to think it will."

"Clear?" Tabitha glanced skeptically out the window as the heavy rain drummed down like a curtain. Thankfully she seemed to catch Midnight's telling glare and immediately coughed. "Yeah, I heard that too. And it definitely looks lighter."

"Totally," Midnight seconded as she grabbed the lunch her mom had made and dragged Tabitha toward the front door. It took them several moments to put on raincoats and pick up umbrellas before they ventured out into the stinging rain.

The sky was the color of metal, and the sound of car tires splashing through the water filled their ears.

"Don't say it. I messed up about Logan and the date." Tabitha groaned as soon as they were free from the house. "It was the brownie. It's like catnip. I fall for it every time. At least Taylor wasn't around to tease you."

"It's okay," Midnight said as they both raced for the bus shelter, the wind and rain making it difficult to speak. They usually walked to the school, but with the weather so bad, that wasn't an option. "I was going to tell my mom today anyway. Not that I'm sure I should be going. After all, we don't have a clue how to figure this thing out."

"What? No, you can't cancel," Tabitha said as the bus pulled up. They clambered on, water dripping off them as they sat down. "Besides, it's only Wednesday. We have plenty of time. And I did get the face from the mirror."

Midnight nodded. Tabitha had sent her the photograph of the mirror last night, after she'd blown it up and applied several filters. It was just about possible to see a face, but they couldn't tell who it was.

"Plus, there's the button you found. Any progress with that?"

"None," Midnight said as she pulled the silver button out of her pocket. She'd spent the night on the Internet, hoping that she would somehow find information about it. Perhaps that it once belonged to a convicted villain who was now living in Berry (at a location easily accessible for two middle schoolers). Or, at the very least, that it was only sold to people over the age of fifty. Or with brown hair. *Something* to help them narrow things down.

Instead, it just appeared to be an ordinary button.

"Oh." Tabitha didn't look too disappointed as the bus stopped at the school and they clambered off. "Well, luckily, I have a new plan. That rude woman from the museum told me to read it in the newspaper like everyone else, and I realized that was the perfect idea! Mrs. Crown has lots of old *Berry Gazettes* in the archives, and I thought we could go through them to see if anything like this has happened before. Something so old that it isn't on the Internet."

"Wait? So we really *are* going to the library?"

Tabitha looked confused. "I told you that back at your house."

"Yes, but I thought it was a cover. Or code," Midnight said as they reached the building in question. A large notice on the front wall stated that no raincoats or umbrellas were allowed inside, and that wet children would be kicked out immediately. Midnight gulped as she tried to shake the water out of her hair. "In case you've forgotten, Mrs. Crown hates me."

"She doesn't *hate* you," Tabitha said. Mrs. Crown was at the counter returning books, but she looked up as they walked in. She gave Tabitha a smile and nodded to a glass door that led to an off-limits area where Midnight had never been before. The librarian narrowed her eyes as she noticed Midnight.

"What do you call that, then?" Midnight asked in a whisper.

"Okay, so perhaps you're not her favorite person in the world, but at least she's letting you in." Tabitha opened the door to a reveal a room filled with metal shelves from the floor to the ceiling. On the shelves were stacks and stacks of newspapers. They were brown with age, and the musky smell of ink and paper hung in the air.

"I suppose," Midnight said. After an incident last year, when Midnight had discovered a pile of books on the wrong shelf (and she'd pulled them all out and piled them on the floor, like any self-respecting Dewey lover would do), she'd been barred for two weeks. Apparently Mrs. Crown had a memory like an elephant, because she still hadn't forgotten it. "So, what exactly are we looking for?"

"It occurred to me that the Agency of Spectral Protection doesn't even know for certain that this weapon exists. It's just a theory," Tabitha said as they reached the corner with the oldest newspapers. It was off-limits to most students, but Tabitha wasn't most students. Apparently she'd even seen Mrs. Crown smile, though Midnight wasn't sure she believed that.

"Okay. So, how does this help us?" Midnight wasn't sure where her friend was going with the idea.

"Don't you see? They also didn't know about the spectral transformer that George Irongate had built." Tabitha nodded her head as if hoping that would make Midnight understand.

And suddenly she did. She let out a soft gasp. "You think that George might have made another weapon?"

"That's right." Tabitha walked over to the racks of old papers. "And if he did, that might be what we're looking for!"

Midnight scanned the dates until she reached 1875. "This is the year that George Irongate invented his first weapon, according to his diaries. It's a good place to start."

"Hey, not so fast." Tabitha jumped to stop Midnight from touching the newspaper itself. "No wonder Mrs. Crown doesn't trust you. These are archives. Which means we both need to have clean, dry hands."

"Sorry." Midnight followed Tabitha to the sink in the corner of the room. "I didn't realize."

"You're just lucky Mrs. Crown wasn't looking." Tabitha finished drying her hands and showed Midnight how to take the newspaper out and carefully spread it onto the viewing desk. She then collected a newspaper of her own, and they both got to work.

The paper was brittle with age, and the print was tiny. Midnight had to remind herself that she wasn't on a device where she could just increase the size. Then she noticed a large magnifying glass on the table. She reached for it and studied the first page. *Miss Soybean Winner! Fire on Pitt Street! Drink this Vitalizing Tonic!*

"They sure liked their exclamation points back then." Midnight turned the page. By the time she put away the twentieth newspaper, her shoulders were tight and her eyes were beginning to ache. She took off her glasses and was about to reach for another paper when Tabitha let out a small gasp.

"I think I've found something. Look at this. April 5, 1901." Her friend pointed to an article in the paper she'd been studying. Midnight leaned over her shoulder.

Houdini Was Here!

Astonished onlookers didn't know what to say when a four-carat pink diamond, set in an engagement ring, melted in the display cabinet in Berry's oldest jewelry store, Nixon and Wright. Trevor Nixon said that the diamond ring had been commissioned by the mayor, who'd been left heartbroken and angry by the mysterious occurrence! Police haven't been able to shed any light on the disappearance, and if rumors are to be believed, the mayor ordered for the ring to be taken so he could break his engagement.

Below the article was a photograph of three men. It was grainy, making it impossible to see any distinctive features, but the caption underneath named the men as Trevor Nixon, Simon Wright, and their longtime employee, William Irongate.

William Irongate?

Midnight and Tabitha turned to each other.

William was George Irongate's younger brother who was buried at the Irongate mausoleum along with George, his first wife, Mary, and his daughter, Eliza. But Midnight and Tabitha didn't know anything else about him, other than the fact he'd never married. It was entirely possible that he had access to all of George's inventions.

The girls let out a small squeal as Tabitha held up her cell phone and quickly took photographs of the article, the picture, and the date of the newspaper. Finally, they had a clue that wasn't a button.

CHAPTER SIX

"Midnight, how lovely to see you," Tabitha's mom said as the two girls upended their umbrellas at the doorway to Tabitha's house later that day and hurried inside. Unlike Tabitha, who wore mostly black clothes, her mom favored jeans and pastel sweaters. Today's was robin's-egg blue. She was also super nice and didn't even seem to notice when Tabitha got grumpy.

"Thanks, Mrs. Wilson," Midnight said.

"My pleasure." Tabitha's mom beamed as she ushered them in. "You two are soaked. Would you like to dry off while I make you some snacks?"

"We're okay," Tabitha said quickly. "We have loads of homework to do, so we're going to head straight up to my room."

Which wasn't really a lie. Their math teacher had given them pages of work to do, but they'd finished it at lunchtime. Right now, they were going to research William Irongate using Tabitha's numerous genealogy programs.

"Of course. Oh, and Tabitha, Louisa from the club wanted to know if you could join us for doubles. Her sweet daughter's very eager to see you."

"The one who wears pink bows in her hair and talks like a Chipmunk?" Tabitha said, looking mildly disgusted. "I don't think so."

"Well, if you change your mind, let me know," her mom said cheerily as she wandered back to her home office. Once she was gone, Tabitha groaned as they walked to her bedroom.

"I wish my parents would stop trying to drag me to their stupid club. Do I look like a person who wants to play tennis and sit around drinking orange juice on the patio talking about the Gap catalog?"

"Perhaps she just wants to spend time with you."

"Well, then she can come to the cemetery," Tabitha retorted. "Anyway, I don't want to talk about tennis *or* my mom. We need to get to work."

Midnight had contacted Peter, and the team at ASP had gone through all of George Irongate's possessions that had been taken from Miss Appleby's house. They hadn't found any mention of William's personal details. So, the new plan was to keep doing local research for anything connecting William to spectral energy.

The words *needle* and *haystack* came to mind.

The girls hurried up the stairs to Tabitha's bedroom. It was sleek and modern, like the rest of the house, but the walls were covered with posters from old movies that Tabitha kept threatening to make Midnight watch. Yes, she could see ghosts, but that didn't mean she wanted to see people get killed by vampires.

However, while they didn't agree on movies, when it came to working, they got along perfectly. Ten minutes later, Midnight was set up at the base of Tabitha's bed, while her friend was spread out on the floor. They'd agreed that Midnight would do a general search while Tabitha went through the Irongate family tree.

"Okay." Tabitha toyed with her pencil. "We know that William was born in 1858 and died in 1910, so he was about forty years old when he was working in the jewelry store. And potentially stealing from it. Oh, and he never married."

"And we also know George Irongate died in 1895, and that Miss Appleby continued to live in his house. Which means William must've been living somewhere else. If only we could find out where." Midnight typed another search into her laptop.

"Yes, but this is going back one hundred years. Even if we find out, what are the chances that anything would still be there? I know George left behind a secret room," Tabitha said, referring to the hidden study where all of George's inventions had been kept. "But I doubt we'll be so lucky a second time."

"If William did have one of George's weapons, then whoever's using it now must have gotten it from somewhere," Midnight mused.

"Okay, so we'll try your idea of finding out where he lived." Tabitha began to type. Five minutes later, she let out a groan. "I have good news and bad news. He lived in a boardinghouse that was run by a woman named Cecelia Perkins."

"Really?" Midnight's eyes brightened before catching Tabitha's expression. "What's the bad news?"

"It burned down in 1899, just before the robbery," Tabitha said as her mouth tightened. "Why do I know the name Cecelia Perkins?"

"I don't know. Perhaps you've seen her gravestone at the cemetery?"

"No, it's not that," Tabitha said as their cell phones simultaneously began to ring. It was the ghost app, letting them know that somewhere spectral energy was trapped.

"It's at Seven Oaks Mall." Midnight studied the screen as her stomach dropped. Normally when spectral energy was trapped in a public place, she waited until after hours to lessen the chances of being caught. However, the mall was locked up after hours, which meant there was never a good time to go there.

Tabitha's face went pale. "That's risky."

"It's even more risky not to help release it. Especially with what's happening to the Black Stream. Things are crazy enough in Berry right now without making it worse."

"Okay, so we should get going." Tabitha reluctantly shut her MacBook. It was obvious she would prefer to keep researching—and if they wanted to solve the case, they needed to find out more about William Irongate.

Midnight shook her head. "I think you should stay here."

"Life would've been easier if George Irongate had invented a machine to let us be in two places at once," Tabitha said in a wistful voice before nodding her head. "Okay, I'll keep researching, but let me know how everything goes."

"I will." Midnight got to her feet, her mind already planning her course of action. Get CARA. Tell her mom she was babysitting for an hour. Use some of her expense money to get a cab to Seven Oaks. Release spectral energy, and be home in time for dinner. It was tight, but if she hurried, it might just work.

* * *

Midnight gritted her teeth as she pushed her glasses further up her nose. The entire department store was filled with black fog, pulsing like a heartbeat, while people wandered past, oblivious. She'd spent ten minutes trying to locate the source on the lower floor before making her way up the escalator. The high-pitched buzz rang in her ear as she followed the dark tendrils, her knuckles white as she clutched her backpack.

"I swear I haven't worn them before," a familiar voice said. Midnight looked over to see Malie standing in front of a customer service counter. Her dark skin was glowing, and amazing spiral curls were flattened down and held back from her brow by one of Sav's old headbands. She was leaning over the counter, clutching a pair of jeans that looked like the ones she'd been wearing at the museum. "Please, you have to give me a refund."

The clerk was silent, then gave a curt nod. "Very well, but next time there's a stain, we won't be able to do anything."

Midnight looked over with interest. When she'd been friends with Sav and Lucy, she'd tried her hardest to keep up with their belief that new clothes were everything. It's what had led her into working for Miss Appleby—she'd needed the extra money. Of course the irony was that while Midnight had accidentally helped an evil old woman to try to compete, Sav and Lucy had been shoplifting.

"I swear it was there when I bought them." Malie took her money and turned around. At the sight of Midnight, her mouth dropped open. "What are you doing here?"

"Just shopping," Midnight said, trying to act like the entire room wasn't filled with hideous darkness.

"More like spying on me," Malie retorted, two patches of color forming on her cheeks. "And whatever you *think* you just saw, it's not like that. I have money. Lots of it."

"Okay," Midnight said, torn about whether to say anything or not. It was none of her business. Then she caught the strain around Malie's eyes. "But for the record, I know better than anyone how exhausting it is to try to impress Sav and Lucy. If you want my advice, just be yourself."

"As if I'd listen to you. After all, if your advice worked, you would've gone skiing with them. Plus, look at your outfit." Malie gave a dismissive snort and folded her arms so that the plastic bag she was holding was on full display. It was from a costume store at the far end of the mall.

Midnight flinched at the memory of the ski trip she'd been invited to go on before being unceremoniously dumped. And there was nothing wrong with her outfit. She glanced down at the plain jeans and the random T-shirt that she'd put on, topped off with a comfortable hoodie. She'd spent so much time worrying about her clothing when she'd been friends with Sav and Lucy. These days, she enjoyed wearing whatever she wanted.

"I was just trying to help," Midnight said as the spectral energy swirled around them, a low hiss buzzing in her ears.

"Well, I don't need it." Malie patted the bag in her hands. "I have it all under control." Without another word, she stormed out of the department store. The gathering spectral energy shrouded around her like a veil.

Midnight opened her mouth to protest, but before the words could come out, she finally saw the source of the spectral energy. It was coming from a display of headphones. She pushed Malie from her mind and walked over.

A putrid smell hit her nose, and Midnight stiffened as the long mirror that ran behind the display filled with mist. For an instant, a face flashed across the surface before disappearing again.

Ice filled her veins.

Was this another planodiume rupture?

The smell increased, and Midnight tried to hold her breath as she identified the headphones that the energy was trapped in. She reluctantly picked them up and hurried to the counter. Once she'd paid, she raced from the store and through one of the many fire exits to the labyrinth of concrete corridors that wrapped around the mall, hidden by the storefronts.

They were regularly used by security guards, delivery people, and contractors, but thankfully the one she'd chosen was currently empty.

Thick billows of darkness raced up and down her arm, as if trying to scare her. Midnight lifted CARA out of her backpack. A shrill scream rose from the headphones, and the air turned to frost, sending a chill through her bones, while her breath hung in the air. She forced her numb fingers to tighten around CARA.

White light poured out, enveloping the darkness. But instead of breaking up, the light disappeared, blanketed by the dark fingers of spectral energy and accompanied by a curdling scream. Blackness sprayed forward, trying to drag CARA from Midnight's hands, while the floor beneath her rumbled, sending her crashing to the ground.

Midnight scrambled to her feet and tightened her grip on CARA. A blast of blinding light pummeled through the dark fog until finally pale-pink sparks filled the corridor. It was over.

She dropped her arms to her side, fighting to get her breath back, as she pulled out the small device to measure the temperature. In the last two months, she'd faced trapped spectral energy twenty-eight times. But it had never been like that before. Then again, she'd never come up against planodiume ruptures before.

The device beeped to say the readings were complete, and she packed her equipment away.

Peter Gallagher had warned that the more disrupted the Black Stream became, the worse things would get. Was this what he meant? Because if so, the sooner they solved the case, the better.

CHAPTER SEVEN

"A clue, a clue, my kingdom for a clue." Tabitha dramatically waved her banana in the air as she stared at the notebook in front of her. Thankfully, due to their remote location in the cafeteria, no one overheard them. "Gah. This is so frustrating. I spent all night researching, and I'm no closer to finding anything out."

"We have a button." Midnight pushed aside her own paperwork. The downside of all the rules ASP expected her to follow was the mountain of paperwork. And normally, she was a girl who loved paperwork! But between the investigation, school, and trying not to think about the fact she had a date on Saturday, she was finding it hard to focus. "And don't forget the planodiume rupture in the department store."

"A button, and the fact our villain looked at some headphones." Tabitha snorted. "It's embarrassing."

"You didn't even want to do this investigation."

"I know, but now that I've agreed, I have my reputation to consider. What must Peter Gallagher think of me?"

"Probably the same thing he thinks of me," Midnight said. "Besides, it's not like anyone else at the Agency of Spectral Protection has figured it out. Or the police, for that matter."

"That doesn't make it any better. This whole thing is turning into a joke." Tabitha broodingly glanced at the pile of local newspapers on the table. They were filled with ridiculous headlines:

"The Case of the Golden Meltdown!"

"Meltgate!"

"#SaveSweetWednesday"

"If it's a joke, it's not a funny one." Midnight shuddered, hating that anything to do with spectral energy was being covered in the papers.

The only piece of information they'd gleaned from the articles was that a small section of security footage—from five days before the robbery—had been erased. It had left police baffled, but Midnight knew it was most likely when the thief had struck, then destroyed the footage to hide what they'd done.

She'd spoken to Peter Gallagher, and there was no disguising the concern in his voice when she'd described what had happened at the mall. He confirmed from the readings she'd sent over that it was definitely a second planodiume rupture. Which meant the person they were looking for was becoming more dangerous by the minute.

"The agency is going over George Irongate's diaries again in case our theory about him inventing this weapon is correct," Midnight reminded Tabitha. "Until then, we need to find anything that can help."

"Help what?" Logan asked as he slid into the spare chair, causing Midnight and Tabitha to both stiffen. Tabitha was the first to recover as she snapped her notebook shut, while Midnight did the same. He looked at them both before narrowing his eyes. "Oh, I get it. You two are trying to solve the museum mystery."

"What? No. Huh?" Midnight yelped before realizing that she was sounding like a crazy person. "W-why would you say that?"

Logan blinked. "Er, because you have all the newspapers sitting in front of you. Plus, I saw you at the museum on Tuesday, remember? You know, if that's what you *are* doing, I'd love to help. I've been thinking, why did they steal Sweet Wednesday? There were other things in the museum worth more money. So, that's my starting point. It was donated by the Talbot Trust, so I'm going there this afternoon to ask them questions, if you want to tag along."

"Oh, right." Midnight gulped, suddenly wishing she was out releasing spectral energy. It might be scary, but not nearly as scary as this conversation. Because it could lead to rule breaking. And that would be bad. "S-sounds cool, though we're not doing anything like that. Tabitha was just looking at—"

"The obituary columns." Tabitha scooped up the newspapers and hugged them. "Yup. I really am that creepy."

"Okay." Logan glanced from Tabitha to Midnight and coughed. "So, anyway, Midnight, I'm looking forward to Saturday. I've been trying to avoid any reviews in case there are spoilers."

"Yeah, me too," Midnight said, not wanting to admit that she'd been so busy it hadn't even occurred to her to read the reviews. She was saved from replying by the eruption of a food fight at the other end of the cafeteria. Everyone stood up and raced over, while Midnight and Tabitha exchanged a secret look. That had been too close for comfort.

* * *

"Midnight, stop wriggling," her mom said from down on the floor as she tried to get the hem the right length on the bridesmaid dress that Midnight was expected to wear. Not that anyone would be looking at the hem, on account of the fact she'd be wearing a helmet. With horns on top.

Phil had tried to tell her that they were actually spikes, and that contrary to popular belief, Vikings didn't have horns on their helmets. But as far as Midnight could tell, a spike the size of a horn was just as bad.

"Yeah, Midnight. You should wear that on your date." Taylor smirked from her spot on the sofa, where she was busy sending text after text, probably to her boyfriend. While Midnight was going to the wedding dressed as a Viking, Taylor had *somehow* convinced their mom to let her wear something more contemporary. The only thing that had stopped Midnight from refusing to wear the horrible dress she'd been stuck with was that her mom was looking seriously freaked out.

"That's enough, Taylor," her mom chastised. "And Midnight, you need to stay still."

"Sorry." Midnight took a deep breath and tried not to care that the handwoven fabric was tickling her skin, or that it smelled like beetroot.

"It's okay. I'm the one who should be apologizing. I just keep thinking that if I can get everything right, then it will *have* to stop raining," her mom said. "The wedding is in three weeks. It'll stop by then…right?"

"Of course it will," Midnight quickly said. "My science teacher heard it's going to stop tomorrow. Sunshine for the next month."

"Really?" Some of the tension around her mom's mouth lessened as Midnight resumed her position. "That would give the hillside time to dry out."

"Exactly what I've been trying to tell you." Phil walked into the living room, where the dress fitting had been taking place. Then he grinned as he looked at Midnight's outfit. "That looks amazing. Maggie, I can't believe you made it all. You even have tooled leather bracers to protect her arms."

"You noticed?" Midnight's mom let out a happy sigh. And while Midnight was glad in theory that her mom was distracted, nothing could hide the fact that the bracers were foot-long armbands that smelled really bad.

"Of course I noticed." Phil leaned forward and kissed Midnight's mom. "And sorry I'm late. Jerry was supposed to book the hall for next week's reenactment practice, but with everything going on at the museum, he totally forgot. Thankfully, I managed to get us in."

The museum?

"Who's Jerry?" Midnight swung around to face Phil, causing her mom to let out a frustrated yelp.

"You met him at Thanksgiving. Long red beard and goes by the name Ragnor when he's in full armor. He's going to be my best man. He's head of security at the museum."

"Are you serious?" Midnight's mouth dropped open.

"No, Midnight. Phil loves to go around making things up about people," Taylor retorted from the sofa. "Dylan says that people who ask rhetorical questions show a lack of intellect."

Of course he did. Midnight resisted the urge to roll her eyes as she turned back to Phil.

"Does Jerry really work there?"

"Sure does," Phil agreed.

Jerry might be able to give her some answers. Midnight licked her lips and tried to stay calm. "Was he there the day it happened?"

"Yes, though you probably didn't see him because he's based in the security office, monitoring the surveillance system."

"Wow, that's amazing." Midnight grinned before realizing her mom and Phil were looking at her. "Er, I mean, it sounds interesting. Does he know how the security footage was erased?"

"No. They're all still perplexed," Phil said.

"I bet," Midnight agreed, while trying not to act too curious. "So, Tabitha and I were going to write an article on Sweet Wednesday for the school paper, and we'd love to interview him."

"Oh my God. You are such a freak." Taylor's face was a pattern of disgust. "Why can't everyone just let this mystery go? It's stupid."

"So is texting kitten emojis all night," Midnight retorted. "At least what I'm doing is for the greater good."

"A school newspaper that no one reads."

"Taylor, that's enough. And I'm sure plenty of people read the newspaper," her mom said.

"Totally," Midnight said, even though she couldn't remember the last time she'd seen it. Instead, she gave Phil a hopeful look. "Do you think Jerry would talk to us?"

"I'm sure he would. Problem is that he's out of town until next week. Poor guy, his brother was in a car accident, and his health insurance won't pay for his rehabilitation. Jerry's trying to find a new care facility for him."

"Oh, how terrible." Midnight's mom reemerged from the floor, her eyes full of compassion. "Poor Jerry. We must get him over for dinner when he gets back."

"He'd like that," Phil said before turning to Midnight.

"And he'd be happy to answer your questions when he returns."

"Great," Midnight said just as her cell phone beeped. She discreetly glanced at the screen. It was an email from Tabitha.

> I know where all of William Irongate's belongings might be!!! His landlord, Cecelia Perkins, set up another boarding-house—and not only does her great-great-granddaughter, Elsie, still live there, but she donated Cecelia Perkin's quilts to the museum. (Remember Alan showed them to us just before the gold disappeared?) That's why I recognized her name! I got the idea when Logan mentioned that he was going to research the Talbot Trust.

Midnight gasped. Two clues in one night? This was exactly what she'd been looking for. A breakthrough. Something to ensure that the freaky weather, the plan-odiume ruptures, and having to hide information from Logan would soon be in the past.

"Good news?" her mom asked as she walked over to her sewing box and pulled out what looked like a bright-orange fake-fur jacket. Taylor snickered from the sofa and held up her phone to take a photograph. No doubt to send to "Dylan Says." Still, it was going to take more than a bad costume to spoil Midnight's mood.

CHAPTER EIGHT

"Suddenly, I'm not sure this is a great idea," Midnight said on Friday afternoon as they stood outside the boardinghouse where they thought William Irongate had once lived. Tabitha had called Elsie Perkins the previous night and asked if they could do a school report on the place. Elsie had immediately said yes, and now Midnight knew why.

Because the place was creepy. With a capital *C* creepy. Elsie Perkins probably ate children for breakfast.

"I'm sure if it was sunny, it wouldn't look so bad," Tabitha said, but she lacked conviction as they stared at the house. It was covered with dead vines that glistened in the pounding rain. The attic windows stared at them like eyes, and the narrow porch leaned to one side.

"You're kidding, right? It could be covered in unicorns and rainbows, and it would *still* look bad." Midnight hugged her arms close to her chest. "And can I remind you that the last time I went to visit an old woman in her house, she turned out to be evil?"

"Yes, but Miss Appleby's house didn't look creepy. Therefore, your logic is flawed. Besides, don't forget we have this photograph. Elsie Perkins might be able to help us identify who it is," Tabitha said as she took another glance at the photograph of the mirror in the museum. It hadn't turned out as well as they'd hoped, but there was definitely a blurry outline of a face staring out from the mirror. It was too smudged to identify, but Tabitha was right. Elsie Perkins might hold the key.

"Fine. But if we get killed by a freaky old woman, don't say I didn't warn you," Midnight said as the rain pounded on her umbrella.

"Wouldn't dream of it. Anyway, if it was really creepy, our ghost apps would be buzzing." Tabitha purposefully walked up the overgrown path. The door might've been black once, but it was now faded with age, and the brass knocker—in the shape of a gargoyle—was dull and tinged with green. Tabitha gave a resolute knock and then stepped back. Midnight did the same as the door slowly opened to reveal a woman in her mid-thirties with a bright smile and an even brighter red sweater.

"Ah, you must be Tabitha and Midnight. You're both white as sheets. Let me guess…This place freaked you out."

"Er…" Tabitha's lip twitched, as if she was unde-cided on whether to lie or tell the truth. But the woman just grinned.

"It's okay. It freaks me out too. But, come in. My grandmother's in the parlor."

"Grandmother?" Midnight wrinkled her nose. "Aren't we here to see you?"

"Nah, you only get me by default. I'm Ruth. I take care of Elsie. Well, I try to. She can be a bit of a handful at times. I mean, look at this place. It's way too big for her, and maintaining it is a nightmare, but she refuses to move out because she's worried that Reggie won't be able to find her. That's her fiancé, by the way. He died in the Vietnam War, but she keeps forgetting and is waiting for him to come home. Just a head's-up that she talks about him a lot."

Midnight gulped. "If our visit is a bother, then—"

"Goodness no." Ruth shook her head and waved for them to follow her into the house. "She adores having guests, which is why she was so pleased when you called. I do too! I only moved back recently to take care of her, and meeting people has been hard. Come on in."

Midnight had to admit that the inside of the house wasn't nearly as bad as the outside. To the left was a staircase, and to the right was the parlor where an elderly lady with soft curls and wide green eyes was sitting. She looked up as they entered and smiled.

"Hello, girls."

"Hi, Mrs. Perkins," Tabitha said as she quickly introduced themselves. "Thank you so much for letting us visit."

"Don't be silly. Ruth will tell you how much I like visitors. Though we can't be too long. I'm expecting Reggie soon."

Ruth coughed and excused herself from the room.

"We won't take up too much of your time," Midnight said. "We were hoping you could help us with some information about someone who used to live here a long time ago. His name was William Irongate."

"I'm sorry, but I don't know him. Was he friends with my Reggie?" The old woman looked perplexed.

"No." Tabitha shook her head, her black hair falling around her shoulders. "He was a friend of your great-great-grandmother, Cecelia. We think he might have left some of his possessions here."

"You mean all the things in the attic? Like I told that nice person from the museum when they came to collect the quilts, there's all sorts of things up there. Reggie said he'd help me clear it all out. I wonder where he's got to?" Elsie said with a frown.

Midnight and Tabitha looked at each other, their eyes widening.

"Someone from the museum asked about the things in the attic?" Midnight asked. "Did you let them go up?"

"Well, of course, dear. It would be rude not to," Elsie said as her eyes brightened. "Would you like to go up?"

"That would be great," Midnight said. "Also, do you remember the person's name?"

"I'm sorry, dear. I don't. I wonder if Reggie would know. We can ask him when he comes home. Anyway, the attic stairs are on the second floor at the back. When you get back, we can have a tea party."

"Thank you," Tabitha said, even going as far as plastering a smile on her face. It looked weird, but it also let Midnight know her friend liked the old lady. So did Midnight. They followed Elsie's directions up an old wooden staircase. The walls were covered in black-and-white photos, and a dusty chandelier hung from the ceiling. They reached the landing, which was covered in faded carpet. In the hall was a large glass-faced cabinet, but it was half empty, as if the contents had been sold off over time.

At the far end of the hallway, a narrow set of stairs led up to the attic. The door creaked as Midnight and Tabitha pushed it open. They were greeted by towers of boxes and trunks, all covered with white sheets.

Heavy scents of lavender and mothballs filled the air. Midnight flicked on the light, and dust motes danced around them. Tabitha took a photograph of several footprints that were outlined on the floorboards.

Midnight flipped the first sheet back. It was an old trunk filled with fabric and spools of thread. Midnight recalled that Elsie's great-great-grandmother Cecelia had made all the quilts that were donated to the museum.

"I guess it was too much to hope that we'd find something in the first place we looked," Tabitha said, her eyes still bright with excitement. However, after thirty more minutes of fruitless searching, they hadn't found anything more than thirty years old. Definitely not something that had once belonged to William Irongate.

"What if it's in one of the bedrooms?" Midnight mused.

"But she said the person from the museum came up here. We need to keep looking," Tabitha said, pointing to the chipped redbrick chimney. "Remember that story my dad told me about people hiding things around chimneys?"

"It has to be worth a try," Midnight said. When they'd been searching Miss Appleby's house to find a missing part of a weapon, they'd tried it, only to be disappointed.

"Exactly. And look, whoever was here also went over there." Tabitha pointed to the footprints that were still visible on the dusty floor.

The girls didn't speak as they squeezed past the towering boxes. At the base, several bricks were loose. Tabitha squatted down and lifted them out, revealing a small hutch. Inside was a shabby leather box big enough to fit a weapon in.

It was also very similar to the boxes that George Irongate had used to house the other weapons he'd invented.

Tabitha carefully lifted the box out and opened the lid, but whatever had once been there was now gone.

"Whoever came up here must've taken it. Except we still don't know *what* they took." Tabitha frowned, but Midnight was too busy staring at the tiny corner of paper that was poking out of the box's velvet lining.

She used her nail to push back the lining so that she could ease the paper out. Familiar handwriting stared back at her. Her eyes widened.

"This was written by George Irongate."

"Are you sure?" Tabitha leaned over Midnight's shoulder. One page was like a diary entry, and the others were full of detailed plans for how the weapon worked. "I can't even read what it says. The writing's so small."

"I'm positive." Midnight scanned the page. Then she looked up at Tabitha and grinned. "And it looks like we were right. George is writing about his latest invention:

> I have been trying to find some good in the terror that is spectral energy, and I think I have managed it. It can be used as a power source. I've experimented with how to move objects in the same way telegraphs are sent. I have had limited success and am eager to continue my work with the particle realigner. Even more so now that I am soon to be married…

"So he invented it when he still thought that spectral energy was evil, and just before he married Miss Appleby." Tabitha's mouth dropped open. "And then he had so much going on that he might've forgotten all about it. Which means he might not have even noticed if his brother took it."

"Problem is," Midnight said, glancing back at the empty leather box, "we still don't know who has it."

"Yes, but Elsie must!" Tabitha carefully put the box back where it had been. Midnight folded up the letter, and they made their way downstairs.

"Girls, did you find anything belonging to this William Irongate?" the old woman asked.

"We found a letter his brother wrote," Midnight said truthfully. It was one thing to lie to hide the truth about spectral energy from the world, but she wouldn't lie and take something from a person's house. "Would you mind if we kept it?"

"Please, be our guest," Ruth said as she walked in with the tea tray. "I'm slowly trying to get the attic sorted out. That's how we found Cecelia's quilts in the first place. I was secretly hoping to find a pot of gold to restore this place. Still, even though they don't have a high monetary value, the quilts are historically important. That's why we donated them to the museum."

"It's what Reggie would've wanted," Elise chirped.

Midnight's mind raced. "Do you know who came from the museum to collect them?"

"Or what they looked like?" Tabitha piped in.

"I'm sorry. I was out shopping when they came, so

Elsie was on her own. But the person I dealt with was Alan Staunton. He smiled a lot."

"The museum director." Midnight nodded, recalling him from the other day. "So, it could've been him."

"One way to find out." Tabitha searched through her cell phone, swiping at the screen until she held it to Elsie. It was a photograph of Alan standing next to the mining exhibition. "Is this the person who came to the house?"

Elsie peered at it for several moments. "No. I'm sorry, but I've never seen him before in my life."

Midnight swallowed disappointment. So, it wasn't Alan. Tabitha looked equally upset before she brought up another photograph. It was the blurred image from the mirror.

"How about this one?" Tabitha asked, but the old lady shook her head.

"Sorry, my dears. It's too fuzzy to see much."

"That's okay," Midnight said. "Do you remember anything about what they looked like?"

"Well, that's easy. He had brown hair. Or was it blond? And his eyes were just like Reggie's, though a different color. Actually, it might have been a woman," Elsie said, and Ruth let out a soft sigh.

"Sorry, girls," she said in a soft voice. "But if you'd like to leave me your number, I'll let you know if she remembers, or if I find anything else belonging to William Irongate."

"Thanks," Tabitha said, and Midnight tried not to groan. It was like taking one step forward and two steps back. They now knew *what* they were looking for, but they still didn't know *who* they were looking for.

The particle realigner could've been taken by anyone.

CHAPTER NINE

"This is crazy. It will never work," Midnight said as she stared at herself in the mirror on Saturday. A dull-yellow T-shirt and a pair of old jeans stared back at her. As for her hair? Don't get me started, she thought. She took off her glasses so she could avoid looking at herself anymore. "I shouldn't even be going on a date. I should cancel."

"No way." Tabitha looked up from her spot on Midnight's bed.

"But we've still got so much to do," Midnight said. Yesterday after they'd returned from Elsie's house, she'd scanned the letter and sent it to Peter Gallagher. The

ASP technicians were already trying to replicate George's design, based on his drawings and descriptions, in hope of understanding the best way to stop it. Midnight and Tabitha had also left several messages for Alan Staunton. He might not be their suspect, but he could tell them who'd collected the quilts from Elsie Perkins's house. He hadn't returned their calls though.

"Actually..." Tabitha coughed. "I've been thinking about that. What if we asked Logan to help us? I mean, the guy's a super genius, and he lives and breathes Sherlock Holmes. Don't forget he's the one who accidentally helped us find Elsie by mentioning the Talbot Trust. Think how much easier it would be if we had someone who actually knew what they were doing."

"No way." Midnight shook her head. She'd forgotten that she didn't have her glasses on, and the world blurred in front of her. "That's the worst idea ever. Not just because of my spreadsheet, but because of ASP rules. There's a whole chapter on how any civilian needs to be fully vetted by the head office before spectral energy can be discussed with them. Not to mention all the forms that need to be filled out."

"Don't remind me," Tabitha said with a shudder.

After Peter had approached them both about working for ASP, they'd each been given pages of paperwork to complete while the agency ran background checks on them. Not that there was much to check, since they were both only twelve years old.

"But Logan wouldn't mind some forms. So. What's the real problem?"

Midnight sighed. "I'm not sure I want Logan to know that I'm different."

"Has it ever occurred to you that the reason he likes you is because you *are* different?" Tabitha pointed out before holding up her hands in frustration. "And relax. It was just an idea."

A very bad idea.

Midnight still didn't feel comfortable with people knowing what she did. That she could see things others couldn't. What if they weren't as cool and understanding as Tabitha had been?

"Does that mean I can cancel?" she asked in a hopeful voice, but Tabitha shook her head.

"No way. Besides, have you considered that whoever

stole the particle realigner might not use it again? Perhaps it was just a one-time thing. I mean, there haven't been any more reports of disappearing artifacts. And while the rain hasn't stopped completely, I think it's lighter than it was."

Midnight crossed her fingers. "You really think that's a possibility?"

"Sure. And it also means you have no excuse about this date. Though, will you hate me if I tell you that your outfit looks like it's gone three rounds with some spectral energy?"

"That's because it has. I've just realized all my clothes belong to Protector Midnight, and I forgot to get anything for Regular Midnight. Taylor and Malie were right."

"I highly doubt that." Tabitha got to her feet. "Not that I know what you're talking about."

"They've both commented on my clothing in the last week." Midnight glanced at the time. Two hours and counting until she was meant to meet Logan. Tabitha didn't answer. Instead, she walked to the closet and began to fumble through it before emerging with a large carrier bag, which she unceremoniously dumped onto the bed.

A tangle of T-shirts and jackets and jeans spilled out like a color explosion.

"What about this stuff?" Tabitha asked as she began to sort through it.

"That's everything I ever bought while I was hanging out with Sav and Lucy. It feels tainted, which is why I put it at the back of the closet. The clothes remind me of how many mistakes I made when I was trying to fit in."

"Look, I get it." Tabitha held up a pair of apple-green jeans and a pale-pink sweater with a picture of a cat on it. "And I don't want you to think that I'm in *any way* endorsing the color pink. But you have nice things here, so why not wear them and create better memories? Some Regular Midnight memories."

"You do realize you're telling me to wear clothes that you personally hate," Midnight said in surprise. But Tabitha shrugged.

"My signature style is epically awesome, but I don't expect you to dress the same way. Trust me, not everyone can rock double black! And speaking of which, how do I look for my cemetery tour?" Tabitha asked as she spun around. She had on black jeans with Doc Martens poking out below, and her black T-shirt was covered in Day of the Dead skulls. She'd even broken with tradition and was wearing a denim jacket over the top of it.

She looked amazing. And one hundred percent Tabitha.

"You look like Queen of the Underworld. In the best possible way," Midnight said, and Tabitha grinned.

"Excellent. Exactly the look I was going for."

"I still can't believe you're giving Tyson Carl a tour of the cemetery."

"In the rain." Tabitha flashed a gleam of a smile. "And if I get the faintest hint that he's there because of some kind of bet, I'll take him to the Pettigrew mausoleum. It's practically a mud field to get there."

"No way would he be doing it because of a bet." Midnight shook her head. "For starters, Logan's his best friend. Logan would never let him do something like that. I think Tyson likes you. Question is, do you like him?"

"I'll see how he handles himself," Tabitha said, refusing to be drawn in. Instead, she studied Midnight's face. "Now, go get changed, and then we can talk lip gloss."

"Who are you?" Midnight blinked, then grinned. "But thanks."

"Don't mention it." Tabitha shrugged. "Besides, the sooner we're both ready, the sooner we can get back to researching.

* * *

"That was amazing," Logan said as the end credits ran and the lights in the theater flickered back on. Everyone else had started to leave the theater, but he and Midnight had stayed where they were, since the director always put an extra clip reel at the end.

"It was," Midnight agreed as she reluctantly stood up. And it wasn't just the movie. She'd also managed to eat popcorn without spilling it all over herself, and she hadn't come close to blurting out anything that she shouldn't. Oh, and Logan looked supercute in a blue hoodie. "It sure beats going to the cemetery in the rain."

"Totally." Logan gave a vigorous nod of his head as they both walked to the coffee shop where they'd arranged to meet his mom, who was coming in fifteen minutes. They found a table and sat down. "I was surprised when Tyson told me what they were doing."

"Why?" Midnight stiffened. "Are you saying that he only asked her for a joke?"

"What?" Logan blinked. "No way would he do that. I just meant a cemetery's a weird place to go. I'd much rather hang out in a dry movie theater."

"Even if you were looking for clues?" Midnight said and then regretted it, because the last time they'd talked about solving mysteries, she'd lied to him and pretended that she wasn't interested. "Forget I said that."

"It's cool. You're right. I bet Sherlock Holmes wouldn't be put off by a little bit of rain. Or tombstones," he said before taking a deep breath. "And I wanted to apologize for the other day in the cafeteria. I don't know why I assumed you and Tabitha were trying to figure out what had happened to Sweet Wednesday. I forget not everyone's into the same geeky things I am."

"It's not geeky," Midnight said, trying to keep her voice even. Then she paused. Just because it was against the rules to talk about what she did with an unvetted civilian, that didn't mean she couldn't ask him how his own investigation was going. "So, have you found anything interesting in your research?"

He licked his lips as if trying to decide if she was serious. "Depends on your version of 'interesting.' My parents think I'm crazy to try to figure it out if the police can't."

"I don't think it's crazy," Midnight said as she cautiously leaned forward. "So, what kind of things have you discovered?"

"Okay, so you know a small section of security footage was erased from the museum?" he said, and when Midnight nodded in agreement, he continued. "Well, before it was destroyed there were big, black marks on it, making it impossible to see anyone. The guards thought it was glitch, until it was erased altogether."

"I didn't know that," Midnight croaked. For the black marks to show up on a photograph or image meant someone had been exposed to huge amounts of planodium. It also meant there was a very dangerous person walking around Berry right now.

"Yeah, not many people do. One of the cleaners told me." Logan grinned before running a hand through his hair. "Not that I know what it means. But still, it feels like a clue."

"It sure does," Midnight said, hating that she couldn't tell him he was closer than he knew. "S-so, have you found out anything else?"

"A few things. Do you want to see?" he said.

"Um, sure."

"Cool. At first I was trying to keep track of everything by date, but then I realized that was crazy since I didn't know the real timeline. So, now I'm using a mind map, where I put the main idea in the middle and then have all the different clues and events set off around it. That way, I can visually see how they might fit in," he explained as he carefully took a large piece of paper from his pocket and spread it out on the table.

In the middle were the words *Berry Museum* with a big circle drawn around them, and radiating out like branches of a tree were numerous lines with different clues written at the end of them. The security footage was there, followed by another line listing the names of all the guards and everyone else who worked at the museum. Along with Alan were Malie's mom, who worked in the gift store; Phil's friend Jerry; and even the rude woman from the front desk.

Other clues were shown there too. Elsie Perkins had her own little bubble, as did all the other people who'd made donations to the museum in the last three months. The mind map really was a work of art.

Midnight had never met anyone else who even knew what a mind map was, let along used one. He'd added colors and lines, making it look like a road map. A really beautiful road map. How did she not know he liked organizing things?

"Logan, this is amazing."

"You really think so?" His cheeks colored. "Because I know you love spreadsheets too. I figured you might think it wasn't good enough."

"Are you kidding me?" Midnight continued to stare at the intricate lines spreading out across the page and then back at him. "I think it's cool."

"Me too," he admitted. "And it's really been a game changer. That's how I had the idea to talk to the Talbots about the donated Sweet Wednesday. Not that I ended up with any extra information. Next week I'm going to see Elsie Perkins because she also donated some quilts to the exhibition."

"Don't bother—" Midnight caught herself. "Er, I mean, it sounds like it would be a hassle to go to see her. But I guess that's what it's all about."

He looked hurt. "Yeah, I guess. Maybe I'm just wasting my time?"

Midnight winced. "That's so not what I meant. I think what you're doing is great," she said, since it was thanks to his suggestion that she and Tabitha had found their first big clue.

She hated the idea of him knowing that she was different, but it was tempting to have someone who actually knew what they were doing on their team. And perhaps she didn't have to tell him everything? Just part of it?

She opened her mouth to speak, but before the words could come out, a thin strand of pink fog danced around the empty chair at their table. Midnight choked. The only other times she'd seen pink fog was like this was when the spirit of Eliza Irongate had tried to warn her about Miss Appleby.

So why was she here now?

To stop her from telling Logan the truth.

Because it was against the rules, and Eliza had been killed by a woman who broke the rules.

To remind Midnight that she needed to focus on stopping whoever was draining the Black Stream.

Besides, if she told Logan, and that somehow messed up the investigation, she might ruin everything. The villain wouldn't be found. It would continue to rain. Her mom's wedding would be a disaster, and Peter Gallagher would probably kick her out of the Agency.

"Midnight." Logan studied her face, his dark eyes serious. "Have I done something to upset you?"

"N-no." She quickly shook her head, still annoyed she'd come so close to messing up. "I just have a lot on my mind. Oh, look, here's your mom."

"Right," he said, not quite returning her gaze as they both stood up. Midnight winced. The sooner she solved this case, the sooner things between her and Logan could go back to normal.

CHAPTER TEN

"Ah, she's awake!" Midnight's mom looked up from the newspaper she'd been reading in the kitchen's soft morning light.

"It's not that late," Midnight protested as she stifled a yawn. After her disastrous date that had almost ended in her breaking about six thousand ASP rules, she'd spent the rest of the night trying to figure out why the spirit of Eliza Irongate had visited her. Unsurprisingly, she hadn't discovered anything.

Midnight looked around and realized that the kitchen was full of people and cakes. The cakes she was pleased about, but the people were Taylor and Dylan, which made her less thrilled. "What's going on?"

"Mom's getting married. In case it's slipped your mind." Taylor's bangs had grown out, and her blond hair was pushed back behind her ears. The jeans she'd spent four weeks' allowance on were covered in rips. Dylan's hair was dark and his eyes were green (Midnight didn't care *what* Taylor said, they did *not* look like emeralds), and his own jeans were equally slashed.

"We're tasting wedding cakes," her mom explained as she folded up the newspaper and got to her feet.

"That's today?" Midnight said, feeling a slither of guilt. Taylor was right. It had *completely* slipped her mind. Which showed just how distracted she was, since putting things into her calendar was usually her favorite task in the world. "I'm so sorry that I forgot."

"And kept us waiting half an hour," Taylor said before turning to Dylan. "You're so lucky to be an only child."

Midnight ignored her and looked at her mom. "You should've woken me. I didn't mean to keep you waiting."

"Taylor's just teasing you. We only just got back from the bakery, and Phil's not even here yet. Besides, you had your big date yesterday. You're allowed to sleep in."

Midnight's cheeks burned. Her mom had asked her loads of questions yesterday, none of which she could quite answer. After all, it was hard to know how the date went when half the things that Logan talked about were things that Midnight wasn't technically allowed to discuss.

"These sure look good, Maggie. You don't mind if I call you Maggie, do you?" Dylan said as he lounged on one of the wooden kitchen chairs like he owned the place.

"Of course not." Her mom smiled as if there was nothing weird about the conversation. Dylan gave her a thumbs-up before turning to Midnight.

"And hey, Midnight. How's school going?"

"Fine, thank you," Midnight said, hoping she sounded polite. It wasn't that she disliked Dylan for anything in particular. But Taylor doted on him so much that it was nauseating. Then again, it was hardly his fault. "You know what middle school's like," she added with a shrug.

"Please. Dylan's a senior. He's probably forgotten all about middle school," Taylor retorted as she draped her arm over his shoulder. Dylan let out a strangled sigh.

"I wish I didn't remember. Middle school's the worst.

If you're surviving, you're doing a good job," he said, and Midnight's animosity faded. "Then again, senior year's a nightmare too. So much pressure on which college to go to."

"Well, considering you're brilliant, you'll have your pick," Taylor chimed in.

"Except I still have no idea what I want to do, which is why I wanted to take a gap year."

"A gap year? I'm not sure I know what that means." Her mom's brow wrinkled as she looked up from where she was setting out plates and forks.

"It's when you take a year off before you study. Go traveling, see the world, and have some fun. Unfortunately, my folks won't even consider it," Dylan explained. "I mean, what's the point of going to college when I don't even know what I want to do?"

"Have you tried talking to them about how you feel?"

"Until I'm blue in the face." Dylan sounded bitter. "Unfortunately, my parents aren't quite as cool as you are, Maggie. I wish they were."

"I'm sure you'll find a solution," Midnight's mom said just as Phil walked into the kitchen. Her face immediately brightened as Phil caught her around the waist and kissed her on the mouth. Midnight looked away, and even Taylor let out a vaguely disgusted snort.

"So sorry I'm late. I hope you saved me some cake," Phil said. He was wearing a leather vest, a huge belt almost as big as his arm, a pair of soft leather shoes, and strips of material wrapped around his legs that Midnight now knew were winingas. At one time, seeing Phil dressed as a Viking was the weirdest part of her life. These days, it barely registered.

"We haven't started yet." Her mom giggled, smoothing down the chain mail on his chest. "I have a coconut, lemon, and cacao, a ginger and orange, or a blueberry vegan cheesecake. Plates are here, and don't forget to leave room for lunch."

Midnight grinned. Usually the only time she got cake was when she was at Tabitha's house, so she made sure she took an extra big piece of each. Fifteen minutes later, everyone had decided that the coconut, lemon, and cacao was a clear winner, and her mom was emailing the bakery while Phil washed the plates.

"By the way, Midnight. I spoke to Jerry today, and he's happy to help with the article. He's back in town on

Thursday, and we're meeting at the practice hall in the afternoon. Just come along any time after five."

"Oh wow. Thank you," Midnight said, swallowing the absurd wish to tell Logan about it.

"What's this for?" Dylan looked up from his cell phone with interest.

"Oh, it's some lame article Midnight and her friend are doing about that stupid piece of gold," Taylor said grumpily. Though Midnight wondered if her sister was really annoyed because she'd discovered her boyfriend might go traveling for a year.

"It's not lame," Midnight said.

"Whatever." Dylan shrugged, looking bored by the conversation. So much for Midnight thinking that he wasn't that bad. She opened her mouth to reply, but before she could, the pots hanging over the stove rattled.

The neighbor's dog started to howl, and the floor shook as if it were a boat on the sea.

"It's a tremor," Phil said as he dropped to his knees. "Everyone needs to get under the table and hold on to a leg."

Phil's voice was so commanding that everyone

immediately did as he said, crawling their way to the large scrubbed-pine table as the earth continued to shake and roll beneath them. Taylor's face was leached of color, and her mom's huge eyes were filled with worry—no doubt thinking about whether to cancel the wedding.

Dylan brought up an earthquake app on his cell phone, telling them it should be fine because the epicenter was twenty miles away and the quake only registered three on the Richter scale.

"Hear that?" Taylor said in a wobbly voice as the tremors finally stopped. "Dylan says it will be okay."

But, as Midnight crawled back out from under the table, all thoughts of Dylan were pushed to the back of her mind. Whoever had the particle realigner was clearly still using it, and unless she found them very soon, there would be more earthquakes to come.

* * *

"Midnight Reynolds, is there a reason why you're asleep in my class?" Miss Anderson, her English teacher, asked on Monday morning. Midnight sat up with a jolt as laughter echoed around the room.

Actually, there were several reasons.

She was a ghost protector doubling as a detective. And doing a bad job of it. After the cake tasting, she and Tabitha had increased their efforts to figure out who'd taken the particle realigner. Oh, and after more tremors, the ghost app had gone off at five o'clock in the morning.

Midnight had been forced to sneak out of the house and go to the pizza parlor on Winchester Road. The whole way there, she'd been hoping she'd find just a good, old regular case of spectral energy. But when she'd arrived, the same putrid smell greeted her as a trash can in the back alley shook with fury at her approach.

She'd needed more than twenty minutes to release the energy, and the readings confirmed another rupture. Which meant that their villain not only liked looking at headphones at Laine's Department Store but also ate pizza.

None of which she could tell her teacher.

"Sorry." She stifled a yawn and then spent the rest of the class pinching her arm to stay awake.

"You okay?" Tabitha asked as they hurried to the library to continue their research.

"Yes, just tired," Midnight said as they rounded the corner and almost bumped into Tyson, who was standing by a locker. Tabitha dragged Midnight back around the corner.

They'd discussed Tabitha's date at length yesterday while they'd been going over all their research notes, and it seemed obvious that Tabitha and Tyson weren't a match made in heaven. Then again, Midnight was starting to wonder if she and Logan were any better. Yes, she liked him. A lot. But what was the point when she couldn't be honest about who she was and what she did? It was like being on tenterhooks the entire time.

"Did you want to speak to him?" Midnight whispered, but Tabitha shook her head and stepped back against the wall.

"No, there's no point. Do you know he freaked out when I told him that the entire Hatten family had been killed by a cholera epidemic? It's not like I showed him pictures or anything, even though I have loads."

"You were very restrained." Midnight tried not to giggle at her friend's outrage.

"Besides, I forgot to tell you that he kept asking about the Irongate mausoleum."

"What?" Midnight blinked. "You don't think he knows anything, do you?"

Tabitha shook her head. "No, but it was weird. He said a friend had mentioned it to him a few weeks ago, and he was curious to see it. I mean, apart from all of Miss Appleby's other flaws, her choice in mausoleums was pretty bad. It's not nearly as fancy as some of the other ones there. Take the Ashdown one. Now *that's* a mausoleum."

"Right." Midnight nodded, trying not to smile. However, the smile quickly faded as they reached the library door. Mrs. Crown was guarding it like a three-headed dog. There were also several posters up about what to do in an earthquake.

"You can only come in if you're not wet. Oh, and no phones. Can you believe that yesterday someone tried to order a pizza and have it delivered here?" The librarian narrowed her eyes, searching their shoulders for water. After what seemed like hours, she gave a curt nod. "Cleared."

"I swear she's a second away from retinal scanners," Midnight said after they'd handed in their phones and hurried through before the librarian could change her mind.

"She's just protecting the books. You know how stupid kids can be," Tabitha said in a serious voice. She took her MacBook out of her backpack and stared at the blurry photograph they had from the mirror. It was still their only real clue of what the villain looked like, and they still hadn't heard back from Alan at the museum.

"Are you sure there's nothing else we can do to bring the face into focus?"

Tabitha shook her head. "I've been discussing it with ASP, and they haven't had any more luck than we have."

"It's so annoying. Still, we will be seeing Phil's friend Jerry on Thursday. Hopefully he can tell us something."

"Sure. Of course, there's another idea." Tabitha put the photograph down and held up her pad. There was a neat list of everything they knew, including the latest piece of information. The pink fog that had shown up yesterday. "I still think that we should consider asking Logan to help us. You could speak to Peter Gallagher about it."

"You know what the rules say." Midnight shook her head. "Plus, when I tried to casually ask him, that's when Eliza showed up. It's obviously a bad idea."

"What if she wasn't there to stop you? What if she was trying to nudge you into asking him?"

"It's impossible to say." Midnight frowned. Unlike the ghost movies where specters actually took shapes and spoke in a voice, Midnight had only seen Eliza's face once. The other times, it had just been fog, and she'd been left to guess what Eliza had been trying to tell her.

"Which is all the more reason to speak to Peter. The fact that ASP haven't had any more success than we have might mean they'll say yes, so it won't be like you're breaking any rules." Tabitha took a deep breath. "I know you're worried that Logan might judge you, but I think we're running out of options. Just look at your spreadsheet for opportunity, motive, and means. It's all empty. We have nothing."

Midnight opened her mouth and then shut it again.

Deep down, she knew Tabitha was right. Between them, they were great at research and organizing their time, but solving mysteries was beyond them.

She let out a sigh. "Fine. I'll call him."

CHAPTER ELEVEN

"I'm sorry, I can't authorize that. We'd have to do a full background check and then train him in the appropriate protocol," Peter Gallagher said the following morning as Midnight stood outside the school. He was calling from Australia, and he sounded tired. It also didn't sound like he was going to change his mind. "I know this might seem unfair, but we have these rules for a reason. To prevent people from finding out what we do and creating hysteria. And to stop them from getting hurt. I hope you understand."

"I do." She tried to hide her disappointment. Even though she was scared of Logan finding out the truth about her, she was even more scared of what would happen if they didn't catch the villain soon.

Whatever was happening with the Black Stream was causing more and more spectral energy to get trapped in objects. And the worry lines around her mom's mouth deepened every time she looked out the window. If Logan could help, it seemed crazy not to let him.

"Okay, well, I have a crisis on the Sydney Harbour Bridge that I need to deal with. Let me know as soon as you speak to the head of security for the museum."

"I will." Midnight put her phone away and walked over to Tabitha, whose face twisted into a frown. "You okay?"

"Apart from seeing something that I can *never* unsee? Then yeah, I'm fine."

"What are you talking about?" Midnight said before spotting a growing crowd over by the basketball court. She pressed her glasses further up her nose, more out of habit than anything else. The rain had stopped, leaving the air thick and heavy like soup, but through the gloom she spotted Malie wearing some kind of rainbow-colored cosplay outfit. Her amazing hair was pulled away from her face, and she had a pink rhinestone tiara perched on her head. Next to her, Sav and Lucy were in similar outfits and hairstyles, but with different colored tiaras.

"It's like My Little Pony puked up on them." Tabitha shielded her eyes as if the bright colors were hurting her. "The thing I want to know is *why?*"

"Actually, I bet I know! Remember, I saw Malie at the mall the other day. She was returning something, and I tried to talk to her about being herself around Sav and Lucy."

Tabitha's eyes flashed. "And she laughed at you."

"I know, but I can't hate her for that. After all, I was exactly the same when I was with them. They suck you into their weird world. But, remember I told you that she had a costume rental bag in her hand and said she had a plan?"

Tabitha gasped in understanding. "Bad cosplay was her plan? Wow. Now I remember why I never wanted to be popular."

Midnight laughed as she linked arms with her friend and they walked away from the growing crowd. "Yeah, I'm now starting to think I got let off easy when I was with them. The worst I had to do was dress up as a mouse."

"At least a mouse has some dignity," Tabitha said as they reached the school entrance. "Anyway, enough of them. What did Peter Gallagher say?"

Midnight's smile faded. "He said no. I'm really sorry. I swear I tried. I even told him how Mr. Alexander thinks that Logan will end up at MIT because he's so smart. But Peter just kept talking about paperwork and why it was a bad idea."

"A worse idea than letting some crazy person run around our town using spectral energy to steal things?" Tabitha's scowl was so deep that a seventh grader walking toward them turned and ran in the other direction. On any other day it would've been funny. But right now, Midnight didn't feel like laughing.

"I know it's not ideal," she said as they reached the library. There was no sign of Mrs. Crown so they both headed for their favorite table, only to discover Logan was sitting at it. He was leaning forward, his dark hair a tangled mess as he studied something on his laptop, while Tyson sat next to him, tapping out a drumbeat with his fingers.

Midnight and Tabitha looked at each other and darted behind a cart of books that needed to be shelved.

"Okay, it's not like we're really avoiding them." Tabitha dropped to her knees so she was out of sight.

"Exactly," Midnight agreed as she tucked her knees up and hugged them. "We're just choosing to take a break before we go any further." Then she let out a groan. "We're the worst, aren't we?"

"Under normal circumstances, I'd say yes," Tabitha's shoulders slumped. "But considering we're not allowed to mention anything to Logan, it's probably safest this way. And, since Tyson's *always* with Logan, we're just being practical."

"Thanks for not making me feel bad." Midnight gave her friend a grateful smile and twisted around so she could peer through the books. She blinked. Logan was gone, but Tyson was still there. Deep in conversation with Malie who, close up, looked even crazier with the strange rainbow-colored princess dress and tiara. "Okay, that's weird."

"What's weird?" Tabitha asked before poking her head through the books. Her mouth dropped open. "That *is* weird. I didn't know they were friends."

"I'm pretty sure Sav and Lucy don't either." Midnight

noticed the way Malie kept twisting and turning, as if checking that no one could see them. "I wonder what they're talking about?"

"No idea, but I wish I could lip-read," Tabitha said, two balls of color forming on her cheeks. Midnight studied her with interest.

"Are you okay?"

"Of course I am. Never better," Tabitha snapped, her gaze still firmly fixed on Tyson and Malie. Then she began to crawl toward the bookshelves, signaling for Midnight to follow her.

"What's going on?" Midnight asked as they reached the safety of the stacks and stood back up.

"Okay, so you know how I was saying that I didn't like Tyson and that we're the total opposite of each other?"

"Er, yeah," Midnight said before widening her eyes. "You *do* like him!"

"Shhh." Tabitha hissed. "It's bad enough that I like him without anyone finding out. Especially if he and Malie have a thing together."

"Just because they're speaking doesn't mean they have a thing. They could be talking about the weather. Math homework. The gold that disappeared. Actually, that could be it. Remember her mom works in the gift store at the museum. Logan had it on his mind map. Perhaps he wanted Tyson to ask her a few questions, so—" Midnight said before Tabitha cut her off, her eyes wide like saucers.

"Wait. Why did we forget that Malie's mom works at the museum? It should've been on our list."

"Which proves why Logan's a better detective than we'll ever be," Midnight said.

"Or, because she knows more than she's letting on." Tabitha's voice lowered to a whisper. "What if she's the reason Tyson wanted to know so much about the Irongate mausoleum?"

"That makes no sense. She's new to town, and there's no reason for her to even know who the Irongates are." Midnight wrinkled her nose, then gasped. "Unless she knows exactly who they are. Who William Irongate is."

The two girls stared at each other.

"Is it possible?" Tabitha croaked as they peered around the corner again. Malie's face was knit in a fierce, warrior-like expression. "Oh yeah. It's possible."

"Okay, let's think this thing through. Her mom works

at the museum, so she might have known about the donation. Not to mention that it would give Malie access to the place." Midnight held up one finger.

"When she first came to the school, she was doing loads of local history research. Mrs. Crown even let her use the newspaper archives a couple of times. She could've found the article about disappearing jewelry and somehow linked it to William Irongate." Tabitha held up two fingers.

"She was right next to the planodiume rupture at the mall," Midnight said, raising a third finger.

"And don't forget the most important thing of all," Tabitha said as she narrowed her eyes and raised a fourth finger in the air. "She's desperate to fit in with Sav and Lucy, and we both know that costs money. Lots of money."

Midnight gasped. "When I saw her at the mall, she said she'd soon have lots of money. This gives her motive, means, and opportunity. Now we just have to prove it."

A slow smile spread out on Tabitha's face. "I have an idea. Remember how Logan discovered that some of the security footage had been filled with black smudges?

Well, he might not know what caused it, but we do. Because the person in the shot has been exposed to far too much planodiume. Therefore—"

"All we need to do is take a photograph of Malie, and if she's covered in black smudges, we know she's guilty."

"Right." Tabitha nodded as they both reached for their phones and walked out of the stacks so that they could photograph her properly. Instead, they were greeted by an empty space.

Malie was gone.

CHAPTER TWELVE

"Not so fast," Midnight's mom said the following day. "I've hardly seen you, kiddo. We were meant to do your final dress fitting yesterday afternoon."

Midnight—who was in the process of picking up one of the breakfast muffins her mom had piled onto a plate—blinked and reached for her cell phone to check her calendar. Guilt stabbed at her.

"Why didn't you say anything when I sent you a text asking if I could stay out to work with Tabitha?" Midnight said. "I would've come straight back."

"You said it was an assignment, and I don't want your schoolwork to suffer. And I know you've been busy with your babysitting," her mom said, making Midnight feel even worse, since the only assignment she and Tabitha really had was figuring out the best way to take a photo of Malie. They'd mentioned their theory to Peter Gallagher, who said it was imperative that they didn't raise any suspicions until the thief's identity was confirmed and he could get a team dispatched.

"I'm so sorry. Do you want to do it now?" Midnight asked. She didn't want to try on the itchy fabric again, but she also didn't want her mom stressing about the wedding.

"I can't. I have a ton of things to get ready for my next video. I'm filming it tomorrow. Eggplant and pesto lasagna. Plus, I have to drop Taylor at school."

"No you don't." Taylor wandered in, her face glued to her screen as though it was her only source of oxygen. She was holding a helmet. Still not looking up, she walked to the back door. "I'm taking Sunny."

"Wait. What? I thought I was giving you a lift today." Her mom's face filled with concern. Sunny was the bright-yellow Vespa that had once belonged to her mom but had been gathering dust for years before Phil restored it for Taylor. Her sister hadn't been using it much since she'd started dating Dylan. But, for whatever reason, she'd obviously decided to correct that.

"Yes, but then I remembered that I needed to go to Donna's house first and get my red sweater. I mean, it's Wednesday. I always wear my red sweater on Wednesday. She *so* took it on purpose," Taylor said, finally looking up. "Why? What's the problem?"

"The problem is that you've only been driving your bike for two months and this weather's terrible. Not to mention the earthquakes. There was another tremor last night."

"That was hardly anything. And Dylan says the weather is starting to clear, so if you're worried about your wedding, don't be."

"Right now I'm worried about my two daughters. One thinks she can ride her Vespa regardless of the conditions, and the other thinks it's okay to come and go as she pleases."

"But I can ride my Vespa when I want. I have my license," Taylor protested, while giving Midnight a dark look as if it was somehow her fault. "Besides, Dylan says the best way to get confident is to get in as many different experiences as possible. Think of it that way."

"I'd rather not." Her mom folded her arms and narrowed her lips. "In case you've both forgotten, I'm getting married in two weeks, and Midnight, I'd like you to be wearing a dress that fits. As for you, Taylor, I would prefer that you were all in one piece."

"I'm really sorry." Midnight was seriously going to overhaul her spreadsheet so that she didn't miss any wedding-related events in the next two weeks. "Just tell me when you want to do the fitting, and I swear I'll be there. And ditto for anything else you need done."

Her mom's face softened. "Thank you, honey. And sorry for flipping out. The constant rain and these earthquakes have been getting me down. I'm actually starting to think that we should just cancel the whole thing. Perhaps it's a sign that it's too soon?"

Midnight winced. The only thing it was a sign of was that there was an evil person running around Berry and using the souls of the dead to steal things.

"You can't cancel. I'm sure it will stop raining. Plus, you have to get married. You've already written out two hundred place settings—all in runes—for the Viking feast. Isn't that right, Taylor?" Midnight said, but instead of nodding in agreement, her sister was still moodily staring at her phone, sending text message after text message before finally looking up.

"I still don't see what driving Sunny has to do with the wedding," Taylor muttered before putting her helmet on the cluttered kitchen table. "But, if you're going freak out, then fine, you can give me a lift to school."

Personally, Midnight thought that Taylor could take a refresher course in how to be nice, but her mom seemed to buy it. "Thanks, girls."

Midnight waited until her mom's car disappeared down the driveway before pulling on her raincoat and racing to meet Tabitha.

"What took you so long?" her friend complained, her black coat glistening with rain.

"Minor wedding disaster," Midnight explained as they reached one of the large oak trees that lined the avenue leading to the school. They'd picked the spot because it was the way Malie normally walked to school. "My mom's really freaking out. She thinks the rain is a sign she should cancel the wedding."

"All the more reason to get this sorted out. And here comes Malie."

Midnight swiveled as Malie slowly walked down the road, almost buried in a giant raincoat. All they could see were her giant brown eyes and great cheekbones.

Midnight and Tabitha both pressed themselves against the trunk of the tree. Wet branches rubbed against Midnight's face as she waited until Malie was looking in the other direction. Then she held up her cell phone and took a picture. Tabitha did the same. The girls clicked away, each getting several shots before Malie turned the corner and walked into the school grounds.

"Okay, let's see what we have," Tabitha said, her hands shaking as she inspected the photographs. Midnight's own heart was pounding as she looked at the shots on her phone. There was nothing. No black smudges. No solution to their problem. Nothing.

She swallowed and looked to Tabitha for confirmation. It was obvious her photos were the same.

Which meant that even though Malie might have had means, motive, and opportunity, she wasn't the person they were looking for.

* * *

"Okay, so we just have to cast our net wider," Tabitha said at lunchtime. As backup, they'd taken several more candid shots of Malie, but nothing had changed. No hint of a black smudge around the image, which meant she hadn't been stealing souls by draining the Black Stream.

The bell rang, and they reluctantly packed everything away and joined the crowd of students heading down the corridor. There was no sign of their math teacher when they walked into the classroom, and Sav, Lucy, and Malie were sitting in the middle of the room holding court.

"Are you sure you're okay, Sav?" Lucy asked, the grim expression around her mouth at odds with the glittering tiara woven into her hair.

"I'm fine." Sav's voice wobbled. "It was just a shock. I mean, the three of us were just there yesterday. What if it had happened then? Talk about a life-or-death experience."

"What's she going on about now?" Tabitha asked Marty Doyle, who was leaning forward as if he was watching a television show.

"The thing at the country club," Marty said, not bothering to turn. "She really does think the whole world revolves around her, doesn't she?"

"What thing?" Tabitha said in a sharp voice, and this time Marty looked at her with interest.

"Dude, where have you been? There's been another robbery. It happened about half an hour ago."

"What?" Midnight and Tabitha said in unison as they both moved closer to Marty, whose face was now red. "What kind of robbery?"

"The disappearing-in-front-of-your-eyes kind," Marty said before shooing them away. "Now, if you don't mind, this is the part where Savannah's going to re-create how she *might* have fainted if she had in fact been there."

True to his predication, Sav raised a slender hand up to her forehead, but Midnight didn't look. Instead, she dragged Tabitha to the far side of the room. They hadn't bothered to turn their phones back on after leaving the library, and when they did, the ghost app sprang into life. Location, the Berry Hills Country Club.

Midnight scanned the Internet for more information.

Breaking News

Up until now, the small town of Berry, in rural West Virginia, has been famous for its gold-mining history and its trees. But after a bizarre robbery in which the legendary gold nugget Sweet Wednesday literally vanished from sight, curious eyes have been on the town. And not in vain. A second incident at the Berry Hills Country Club has been reported. An eyewitness said, "One minute, the daggers were hanging on the wall, minding their own business, and the next, they were a puddle on the floor. A puddle, I tell you."

One security guard was injured during the incident. Doctors have confirmed the guard is in stable but serious condition in Berry General Hospital.

Experts claim the daggers are worth fifty thousand dollars and are baffled why more valuable pieces were left behind. Even more curious is that this isn't the first time these robberies have taken place. Our investigative journalists have discovered—in a groundbreaking scoop—that several such incidents took place in the 1800s. While the items were never found and the thief was never captured, one has to wonder if Berry is once again being haunted by the ghosts of its past.

Midnight's throat tightened.

A security guard had been injured? Peter Gallagher had predicted that whoever was responsible for the crimes would get more and more dangerous as they were exposed to higher levels of planodiume.

"This is bad," Midnight said to Tabitha. "We have to stop this soon, which means we have to visit your country club."

"I'd hardly call it mine. You know how much I hate that place."

Midnight wrinkled her nose. "I know you hate it, but this isn't something we can ignore. Not only is there trapped spectral energy—and a possible planodiume rupture—but this is our chance to examine the crime scene. And since they'd never let me in on my own, I can't see another way around it."

Tabitha let out a long-suffering sigh. "This is so

unfair. Helping you catch evil, old women who tried to kill me? I'm fine with that. Running around while you release spectral energy? No problem at all. But making me go to the country club? For this, you're going to owe me. Big time."

CHAPTER THIRTEEN

"Girls, this is Louisa, and her daughter, Chloe," Mrs. Wilson said later that afternoon as they stood at Berry Hills Country Club. It was a large sprawling building with a marble foyer, an entire wall dedicated to a fish tank, and tinkling piano music. Large sliding doors led out to a flagstone patio that was glittering with water, while further down was a sodden golf course stained brown from the rain-soaked soil.

The foyer was an intersection of corridors leading to a dining room, a gymnasium, and much to Tabitha's horror, indoor tennis courts. To fit in, Midnight and Tabitha were both wearing white tennis skirts and matching shirts. Turned out that Midnight wasn't the only one with unwanted clothing hidden at the back of the closet.

"Nice to meet you," Midnight said in a polite voice, while Tabitha continued to scowl. It was hard to tell if it was because of the company, or the fact she wasn't wearing black. Either way, Midnight was grateful that they were at the country club.

Now they just had to figure out where the trapped spectral energy was and look for clues.

"You too. And what a delightful name you have, Midnight." Louisa twirled her racket. "Let me guess… That's the time you were born?"

"Something like that." Midnight nodded her head, while Tabitha tugged at her white skirt as if trying to lengthen it. "So, thank you for letting me tag along. I've never been here before."

"You're welcome," Louisa said, then frowned as she looked around the foyer, which was filled with people, all talking in hushed voices. "Though you seem to have caught us on an unusual day. In case you haven't heard, there was a robbery earlier today."

Midnight feigned surprise. "Now that you mention it, I did hear something. Wasn't it like what happened at the museum?"

"That's right." Louisa nodded.

"Actually, Midnight and Tabitha were at the museum when the first robbery happened," Tabitha's mom said as a group of people swarmed past, all demanding to see where the daggers had been hanging. Several police officers were interviewing staff members.

"How extraordinary!" Chloe squeaked, her face going almost as pink as the bows in her hair. Tabitha was right. She *did* sound like a Chipmunk. "Did it really just vanish?"

"Pretty much." Tabitha finally stopped scowling. "It was awesome. Though I'm not sure I believe that the same thing happened here. I mean, the papers make stuff up all the time. I bet they exaggerated just to sell more issues."

"Oh no." Louisa leaned forward and lowered her voice. "I really shouldn't say anything, but I'm friends with the duty manager. And the daggers dripped away, plain as the nose on your face. To make it even stranger, some security footage from five days ago was erased."

Midnight and Tabitha stiffened.

It was the same modus operandi as the museum. Which meant whoever it was had managed to access both places easily. But the girls still had no idea why the villain had taken the daggers, unless they wanted to arm themselves with weapons. It wasn't a comfortable thought.

As to why the villain had taken the time to once again erase the security footage, all Midnight could figure was that they'd destroyed it without bothering to look at it first. Otherwise, they would've known that their image was already blurred beyond recognition. Still, that might work in their favor. The villain didn't know what he or she looked like on film.

"So they really don't know who did it?" Midnight asked in case Louisa had more insider gossip.

"Not a clue," Louisa confirmed. "A security guard tried to touch the daggers—to stop them from melting—and his entire arm was burned. Doctors have no explanation of how it happened, but they've cordoned off the area until further notice."

Tabitha's mom went pale. "I didn't hear that. Is he okay?"

"He's still recovering, though I think police will be speaking to him soon," Louisa said as her cell phone beeped. She studied the screen and then frowned. "Oh no. This is terrible. Our booking's been delayed by half an hour. I suppose we have to make exceptions, considering what's happened."

"We should go and have a drink while we're waiting," Tabitha's mom said.

"Actually." Tabitha coughed. "I'd like to use the restroom first."

"Sure, it's just down the corridor and to the right," Louisa explained. "We'll go and get a table."

"Sounds great," Tabitha said before exchanging looks with Midnight.

"I might use the restroom too," Midnight quickly said before they hurried down the corridor. She tightened her grip on her backpack, where CARA was nestled. The ghost app had been going off all day, and in the end, she'd turned her cell phone off for some peace and quiet. Besides, as soon as she started to search the buildings, she'd find the trapped spectral energy.

"Okay, so since we only have about five minutes, why don't you go look where the daggers melted, and I'll go ask around," Tabitha said. Midnight quickly agreed and hurried away in a random direction, her shoulder sagging from the weight of CARA.

She pressed her glasses up her nose, determined not to miss anything. Especially after talking to Peter Gallagher last night. It was obvious by the tone of his voice that he was increasingly worried about what was happening in Berry. That made two of them. She'd once again ventured Logan's name as a possible way of figuring it out, but he'd simply referred her to page sixty-five:

> All spectral protectors must submit to the rulings of their
> superiors without question.

Midnight walked past a gymnasium. The instructor was shouting out moves while Taylor Swift blasted out. The corridor split in two directions, and she was about to head to the sauna when a familiar buzz slammed into her ears. Her mouth went dry, and she staggered back like she'd been hit.

A woman walking past looked at her in surprise before continuing on her way.

Midnight forced herself to go in the direction of the buzzing. It increased in intensity and the temperature dropped, sending long fingers of black fog crashing into her legs and almost pushing her over with their icy-cold touch.

As she went, she reminded herself that the spectral energy was only acting like that because it was trapped. Scared. Alone. All it wanted was to be released so it could cross over to the Afterglow. To be its true self.

Something Midnight could relate to.

The thought calmed her shaky nerves as she reached the cordoned-off corridor. Police tape was everywhere, along with warning signs. In the distance was the empty wall where the daggers had once hung. But what really hit her were the dark flames swirling around the space. Flickering and pulsing every time someone went near them.

This was different from regular spectral energy *and* the planodiume ruptures she'd been dealing with. A whole other level of different!

Midnight swallowed hard.

Somehow, the dancing fire was powered by spectral energy. And while no one but her could see the flames, they could still be hurt by them. Which is what had happened to the security guard.

Sweat beaded at her brow, and indecision churned in her stomach. She had to clear the trapped energy. But trying to do it while she was so exposed was impossible. She scanned the area and spotted a supply closet almost opposite the blazing flames. Several police were at the end of the corridor, deep in conversation. Midnight crossed her fingers and darted to the closet, scrambling in there before the policemen turned around.

She left the door open just enough so that she could poke CARA out toward the blazing inferno of darkness. White light exploded out, filling the room. The spectral energy howled in protest. Flames danced up to the ceiling, crackling with anger. Midnight kept her arm steady until the hideous fire finally disappeared, replaced by tiny separate entities, and floating away.

She took out the measuring device to collect readings for when she wrote up her report later on. Then she stepped out of the closest and hurried to the restroom so that she could recover without fear of being caught by the police.

Her sneakers scuffed against the bathroom tiles, but Midnight hardly noticed as she splashed cold water on her face. Her hands were shaking, and she glanced at her reflection. Her face was pale and her mouth was tight and her brown hair looked like she'd just crawled through a hedge. She looked every bit as bad as she felt. And now she had to play tennis?

She was about to text Tabitha and tell her what had happened when voices drifted into the room from the outside corridor and the door opened.

It was Malie. Again.

Midnight blinked. How did this keep happening?

"Oh my God. Are you stalking me or something?" Malie demanded as her hands automatically rubbed her temples, where the tiara was sitting on her pulled-back hair. She looked ill.

"Are you okay?" Midnight said.

"I'm fine," Malie snapped before sighing as she pulled off the tiara and untied her hair. Her wild curls sprung out around her like a halo, and it took all of Midnight's willpower not to be jealous of Malie's amazing hair. "There's a piece of wire in this tiara that keeps digging into my scalp. I can see it, but I can't fix it. Go on, you might as well laugh. Or say I told you so and give me a whole freaking speech on how I should just be myself."

"I was going to say that small pliers would probably be best." Midnight looked at the tiny sliver of metal that was poking out the bottom of the tiara. The end was sharp. No wonder Malie had looked so grumpy. "I have some if you'd like to use them."

"You have pliers in your backpack?" Malie's dark eyes filled with uncertainty. "Are you messing with me?"

"Of course not," Midnight said. She also had a carbonic resonator, a laser pointer, and several devices that could change the room temperature if needed. She swung her shoulder to stop Malie from seeing the contents of the backpack as she reached for the blue pencil case where she kept the tools she sometimes needed in her role as spectral protector. "Here you go."

Malie stared at the pliers for a moment before taking them. A moment later, she held them up so she and Midnight could both see the tiny metal nail that had been causing all the problems. She dropped it into the trash can and gave Midnight back the pliers.

"I'm still not sure why you had them—or why you wanted to help me, but thanks."

"It's no big deal," Midnight quickly said. Especially since she'd recently thought Malie was a crazed, money-hungry person who'd do anything to fit in. Including steal souls of the dead. Unfortunately, Midnight couldn't exactly apologize for that, so helping Malie with the tiara was the least she could do.

"I'd better go. Sav and Lucy are waiting for me outside." Malie quickly put her tiara back on, pausing to check it was straight. Then she let out a soft breath. "If you stay in here for a couple of minutes, the coast should be clear. I know that they've been giving you a hard time."

Now it was Midnight's turn to be surprised. "Okay, thanks."

"It's no big deal," Malie echoed Midnight's words and gave her tiara one final glance in the mirror before walking toward the door. "See you around, Midnight."

"Yeah," Midnight said, not quite sure what had just happened. She was still trying to figure it out as she headed back to the art wing, where Tabitha was waiting. Despite the tennis outfit, her friend was smiling.

"There you are. I thought you were never going to get here. Was everything okay?"

"If by okay, you mean was there a wall of spectral fire all around where the daggers had been," Midnight said.

"Are you serious?" Tabitha's face went as white as her tennis outfit while Midnight filled her in. "Thank goodness you managed to release it. You should've texted me."

"I was just about to. But then I got interrupted. You'll never believe by who."

"Sav, Lucy, or Malie?" Tabitha said before confessing. "I saw them too, so I ducked into the sports wing to avoid them. Which means we kind of have them to thank."

Midnight's brow furrowed. "Thank for what?"

"For helping me figure out who our villain is." Tabitha grabbed Midnight's hand and led her over to a tall glass cabinet that ran up the side of the wall.

"Are you serious?" Midnight's heart hammered.

"I'm deadly serious," Tabitha said as she pointed to a photograph in the cabinet. It was for the winner of last year's golf tournament. Lifetime member. Jerry Van Meek. Midnight stared, not quite sure what she was seeing until she noticed the long, red beard. Her mouth dropped open as she turned to Tabitha.

"Phil's best man. Jerry. He's a member here?"

"That's right." Tabitha ticked off her fingers. "So, let's see. He's head of security at the museum *and* a lifetime member here. Oh, and that button you found might have come from his museum uniform. It looked like it was from something like that. Midnight, I think this is our guy."

Midnight's mind sifted through the information, and she frowned. "But he's out of town until tomorrow. Phil said so."

"Yes, but that doesn't mean it's true." Tabitha gave a dismissive wave of her hand. "After all, what better alibi could you have than saying you're out of town? For all we know, he went away to try to fence the gold and then snuck back to steal the daggers. It could all be part of his cunning plan."

"You're right." Midnight nodded, impressed with her friend's use of the word *fenced*. And Tabitha did have a point. If you were going to steal a valuable piece of gold with a weapon powered by the souls of the dead, a little lie was hardly going to bother you. "So tomorrow when we meet him, all we need to do is take a photograph, and we'll have our proof."

"And in the meantime we can research his financial history, just be sure—"

"There you girls are. We were worried you'd gotten lost." Tabitha's mom appeared, followed by Louisa and Chloe. They were all holding tennis rackets. "Anyway, good news. Our court's ready. Let's go have some fun."

Midnight and Tabitha stared at each other and then burst out laughing. *Fun* was hardly the word to describe the game they were about to play, but having finally found their breakthrough made it easier to bear.

CHAPTER FOURTEEN

"Okay, once you take the photograph and confirm he's been affected by planodiume, then you need to contact me immediately, and on no account are you to approach him," Peter Gallagher said from the other end of the phone as Midnight and Tabitha stood outside Berry Community Hall. It was a single-story red building with ivy climbing up the walls, and the continuing rain made it sparkle like a diamond.

"But what if he hurts someone else?" Midnight's fingers tightened around the cell phone. "Should we try to stop him?"

"Absolutely not. And that's an order," Peter said. "The readings you took from the planodiume flames at the country club have just confirmed how dangerous he is. As soon as you positively ID him with the photograph, I'll have a team fly out. They can administer an antidote to the buildup of planodiume in his system."

"Okay, so we take a photograph, and once we can confirm it, I'll let you know," Midnight obediently repeated while next to her, Tabitha shuffled from side to side impatiently.

Midnight put her phone away, and they stepped into the hall to be met by the clanging of steel on steel. Two Vikings held up long swords, while a third person shouted out instructions.

"Guard up. Cover your right. Pivot."

The scuffing of leather shoes against the floorboards rang out as the men parried, and the air was filled with the heady scent of what Midnight now knew was Viking ale.

Phil was in the distance, but Midnight ducked behind a large potted plant before he could see her. Right now, they wanted to take their photos of Jerry. Midnight scanned the hall until she finally saw him. He had broad shoulders and a red beard that covered his chin and a good section of his neck.

Last time she'd met him, his red hair had hung down his back, but now it was plaited and pushed over one shoulder. She nudged Tabitha, and they held up their phones and took several shots. Jerry was oblivious as he took off his helmet, allowing them to get a better photo.

Midnight sucked in her breath as she dared look at the screen.

"Noooo," Tabitha wailed as her fingers scrolled through all the shots. Not one of them had a black smudge on it. "I was so sure it was him. I mean, it made so much sense."

Midnight tried to swallow her own disappointment as she sent Peter Gallagher a text with the bad news. She didn't *want* Phil's best man to be evil, but now that he wasn't, they were back to square one for the third time.

"Midnight, there are you. Come and meet Jerry." Phil waved them over, and the two girls reluctantly walked around the edge of the hall, careful to avoid all the sword-play that was going on. Phil made the introductions and then excused himself as his cell phone rang.

"I hear you're working on an article about the mysterious thefts. I'm happy to talk to you, but please don't mention my name. Alan Staunton has forbidden us from talking to the media," Jerry said with a broad smile, making Midnight feel even worse for suspecting him.

"Of course," she said, recalling the museum director from their school visit. "We don't want to do anything that will get you in trouble."

"Don't worry. I don't really know much. Just that a small portion of footage from five days earlier was smeared with black before mysteriously being erased. It was the weirdest thing."

"That is weird." Midnight nodded since she couldn't exactly tell him the truth about *why* the tape was covered in black. "Do you have any idea who went to Elsie Perkin's house to collect the quilt collection that she donated? We've left a couple of messages with Alan, but he hasn't returned them."

Jerry frowned. "Sorry, I don't know, though I'm happy to look into it. As for Alan, don't take it personally. He isn't returning any calls. I heard he has a lot going on right now."

"If you could find out who collected the quilts, that would be great." Midnight swallowed her disappointment. "Thank you for your help."

"Of course." Jerry grinned. "Phil's always talking about how smart you are. It's my pleasure to help."

"He is?" Midnight's mood improved. If anyone had told her six months ago that she'd care what Phil thought of her, she would've laughed. But now the idea that her mom's fiancé—her future stepdad—thought she was smart, filled her with happiness. Then her mood dropped again. Of course if she didn't figure out what was going on soon, there might not even be a wedding.

"Sure is," Jerry agreed before his mouth dropped open. "Well, I'll be. If that isn't Ruth Perkins."

"Ruth's here?" Tabitha turned as Ruth walked toward them all, a warm smile on her pretty face. As she walked through the hall, all the Vikings stopped what they were doing and stared at her in admiration.

"Midnight, Tabitha, hello. And, wow…Jerry Van Meek. Aren't you a sight?" Ruth's brown eyes widened. "I haven't seen you since senior year."

"Last day of school. You signed my yearbook, kissed

my cheek, and rode off into the sunset. I didn't even know you were back in town," Jerry said, his face going the same shade of red as his beard.

"It's a long story." Ruth dimpled. "But perhaps we can get together sometime and I'll tell you."

"S-sure," Jerry stammered as Midnight and Tabitha exchanged surprised looks. Then he seemed to remember where they were, and he coughed. "Er, so are you here to see Midnight and Tabitha?"

"Actually, I am," Ruth collected herself as she fished around in her purse for something. "When I was cleaning yesterday, I found this, and when I showed it to Elsie, she thought it belonged to the person from the museum who came to see her. Anyway, I thought you girls might be interested, so I called your house and your mom said you were here. I was coming this way so I figured I'd stop in. I'm sure glad I did." The last bit was directed at Jerry, but Midnight and Tabitha were more interested in what she had her in her hand.

It was a silver button.

"I take it by your expression, this means something." Ruth's face lit up.

"We found a similar one in the museum," Midnight said, not bothering to add that it had been in an out-of-bounds section where spectral energy had been trapped in a mirror. "I've been trying to figure out if they belong to some kind of uniform, but I haven't been able to find any information."

"Well, I can help you there," Jerry said, tearing his gaze away from Ruth to glance at the silver button gleaming in the bright lights of the hall. "It's from the country club. See that squiggle there? It's meant to represent a golf club but ended up looking more like a snake. It became a running joke, and these days they're only used on the bellhop uniforms."

Midnight let out a gasp. Whoever had visited Elsie Perkin's house and taken the particle realigner had also been in the museum *and* worked at the country club. She looked at Tabitha, but before they could speak, Phil came jogging toward them.

"Hey, Midnight. I've just been speaking to your mom. She's about to start filming for her latest vlog and wants you in it. She'll throw in your favorite muffins. You too, Tabitha."

"Oh." Midnight's mind whirled. At that moment, the ghost app rang out on her phone, followed seconds later by the one on Tabitha's. They had a new clue to follow up on, and spectral energy to release. She gulped. "A-actually Tabitha and I were going to do a bit more work on the article. Plus, I'm supposed to babysit today."

"Yeah, the article," Tabitha seconded, neither one of them quite able to look Phil in the eye.

"But I'll call Mom and let her know I can't make it. I'm sure she'll understand," Midnight said, reminding herself that letting down her mom over a cooking video was nothing in comparison to saving her wedding day from being washed out.

CHAPTER FIFTEEN

"Ouch." Midnight groaned as she reached for the polishing cloth that she used on CARA. Her body ached from the spectral energy that had been trapped at the back of the movie theater. At least it had just been plain old, regular spectral energy, which seemed like a slow-motion version of the ruptures she'd been dealing with. Thankfully, the howling wind and rain had stopped anyone from walking past the dumpster that she'd been forced to hide behind as she cleared the spectral energy.

While she'd been working, Tabitha had contacted the Berry Hills Country Club and—through means that

Midnight didn't want to examine too closely—had managed to get a list of the eight bellhops who worked there. After that, the girls had decided to call it a day.

Once CARA was clean, Midnight hid her under the bed before writing out her latest report for the agency. It took an hour before she was done. She hit Send, then turned her attention to her spreadsheet. Clashing blocks of color stared back at her.

What had once been a thing of pristine beauty had turned into a big, fat mess of blurred shades. None of it was helped by the ghost app going off all the time, making scheduling even more difficult.

Midnight glanced at her pile of homework as a pale slither of pink fog slid in under her window.

"Eliza?" she whispered.

In reply, the fog danced around the room, then darted under Midnight's bed like it was playing a game of tag.

Midnight bit down on her lip and waited until the fog reemerged. Then she wriggled under the bed and pulled out the boxes she kept hidden there. As well as CARA, there was the ASP rulebook, a small toolbox, and several other particle realigners. The pink fog swirled around them like an atom, so fast that Midnight's hair fluttered back.

"I don't understand what you're trying to tell me," Midnight said. "Is this about Logan?"

The fog swirled faster.

"Or ASP? Are you worried that I'm going to break the rules? Mess up like Miss Appleby did?"

Faster. Faster. Faster.

Frustration stung at her. "Please, Eliza. I don't know what you're trying to say."

Then, just as suddenly, the swirling stopped and the spreadsheet that she'd printed out fluttered to the ground. But before she could ask any questions, there was a knock on the door.

The pink fog disintegrated into nothing.

"Hang on a moment!" Midnight called out while staring at her ASP equipment. She shoved it back under the bed just as her mom poked her head around the corner of the door.

"You okay?" her mom asked, looking tired.

"I'm fine. Just doing my homework." *Definitely not trying to talk to the spirit of a twelve-year-old dead girl.*

"Well, let me know if you need a hand. Her mom paused, as if weighing her words. "I missed you tonight. It would've been fun if you could've been in the video. Still, at least Taylor and Dylan took part."

Midnight shuddered. Even more reason not to have done it.

"I'm sorry too. But thanks for saving me some of it for dinner. And the muffin. We should have this article finished soon."

"Good," her mom said. "But article or not, there's no getting out of tomorrow night's dance practice. And it's full costume, so you'll be able to wear your shield maiden outfit."

"Wouldn't miss it for the world." Midnight made a mental note to ignore any spectral energy until after the practice was over. No wonder her spreadsheet was so blurred.

"Okay, that's great. And now I need to edit the video. I can't wait to see how it turned out."

"Cool." Midnight absently nodded her head and tried not to yawn. Once her mom had gone, she flattened out her spreadsheet to try to figure out what Eliza had been telling her. But all she found was that she'd double-booked herself tomorrow at lunchtime. She wearily changed her schedule and crawled into bed.

* * *

"Oh, look. It's the golden child who doesn't need to participate in any family events," Taylor said by way of greeting the following afternoon. She then stormed out of the room, knocking over a vase of flowers as she went. Midnight lunged to catch it, her aching muscles screaming in protest. It had been a long day at school, and all she wanted to do was eat a snack and collapse. Not deal with sister drama.

She put the vase back on the counter and walked over to the table where her mom and Phil were sitting. Steam rose from their coffee cups, and croissant crumbs were scattered on their empty plates. Her mom had a laptop in front of her.

"What's wrong with Taylor?" Midnight asked. "Don't tell me Dylan doesn't like her new jeans, or some other catastrophe."

"It's nothing like that." Her mom lowered the screen of her laptop, her face worried. "It's that Vespa. I swear I'm not being one of those airplane mothers."

"Airplane?" Midnight wrinkled her brow before groaning. "You mean helicopter or hover moms? And no way are you like that. You're a cool mom."

"I always thought so." Her mom sighed as Phil leaned over and patted her arm.

"It's my fault," he said. "I never should have restored it for her."

"Nonsense, it was a lovely thing to do. The real problem is that Taylor's determined to go to a party tomorrow night. It's an hour away, and she wants to take the Vespa. In this weather, that's just crazy. Not to mention that it's a school night. So I said no. And of course, Dylan said—"

"Please. No, 'Dylan said,'" Midnight begged. "I'm too tired."

Still, the fact that her mom was distracted with Taylor might be a good thing. It might take her mind off the bad weather—or the fact that Midnight had missed so many things lately.

"You're right." Her mom gave her a rueful smile. "And be warned, I'm going to be the same with you. I'm all for letting you girls express your creativity and push boundaries, but putting yourself into dangerous situations is another thing entirely."

"Of course." Midnight crossed her fingers and tried not to think about what her mom would do if she knew about spectral energy and all the things she'd done in the last six months. Definitely time for a subject change. She glanced over to the kitchen bench and noticed all of her mom's cooking things were out. "Are you filming again?"

"Unfortunately, yes. I was using some new editing software and somehow managed to ruin all of yesterday's footage." Then her mom brightened. "I was just about to start. Would you like to be in it?"

Midnight opened her mouth, but before she could think of any excuse, her ghost app went off, quickly followed by a text from Tabitha:

There's been another robbery. Some diamond earrings have melted away. Meet me at Shaw and Co. jewelry store in ten minutes.

"Sorry. Babysitting emergency," Midnight said quickly before catching her mom's frown. "But don't worry. I'll be home in plenty of time for tonight."

"Good. That means I'll have at least one daughter who doesn't hate me," her mom said sadly.

"Taylor doesn't hate you," Phil said, walking over and giving Midnight's mom a long kiss. Midnight grimaced. Definitely time to leave.

CHAPTER SIXTEEN

Shaw and Co. was situated in an impressive gray stone building with a wide front window full of glittering necklaces and earrings. It was also surrounded by rain-soaked policemen and security tape designed to stop anyone from getting inside. Not that there were many onlookers, thanks to the black skies. Thunder rumbled overhead, and Midnight tugged the hood of her raincoat further up.

"How's it going?" she asked Tabitha, who'd been taking a reading of the electromagnetic field levels.

Tabitha tucked back a strand of black hair and frowned. "This is higher than what we had at the museum *or* the country club. And even if it's invisible to everyone else, we know by what happened to the security guard at the country club that it can still hurt them."

"Which means we have to try to get inside so I can use CARA." Midnight pushed her glasses further up her nose and tried to see past the rain and the thick rolls of spectral energy that were spilling out of the building. Through the window, it looked like the place was empty.

Her fingers tightened around her backpack. It had been easy enough at the museum and country club to get to the source of the spectral energy.

But if she didn't try…

"Any ideas on how we can get in?" Tabitha's pale face was filled with worry.

"Not exactly," Midnight said as a red-faced woman holding a bright-yellow umbrella marched over to the policeman.

"Excuse me, Officer. My daughter's engagement ring is in there getting resized, and I need it for tonight. The party's all planned."

"I'm sorry, but no one can cross this line. We're waiting on the forensic team to arrive." The policeman shook his head, his square jaw set in a fixed line. The woman's face got redder, and instead of leaving, she took a step forward.

"That's not good enough. I only need to go in for one minute. It's all paid for. Besides, it's not like anyone was killed. I heard that only one thing was stolen. A pair of diamond earrings."

"I can't comment on an open investigation," the policeman replied, but still the woman didn't leave. Instead she raised her voice louder, which attracted the other officers who'd been protecting the cordoned-off area.

"Is there a problem?" a second officer asked, just as a third one joined them.

Midnight exchanged a silence glance with Tabitha.

Never look an umbrella-holding gift horse in the mouth.

This might be their only chance to get in there.

"For the record, this is the craziest thing we've ever done," Tabitha whispered as they quickly made their way toward the store. Midnight just hoped that their dark raincoats stopped anyone from noticing them.

Sluggish waves of spectral energy rolled out of the store, hissing as the energy tried to wrap itself around them. A high, buzzing noise echoed in Midnight's ear as they stepped inside. A putrid smell clung to the air. Their villain had left behind another planodiume rupture.

Through the angry fog came a howling noise. Pale-blue icy flames leapt out from a freestanding mirror on the counter.

Midnight hated to think what would happen to anyone who touched them.

"Get behind me," she hissed to Tabitha as an almost-translucent flame rushed at them, stopping just inches from where they were standing.

"Where is it coming from?" Tabitha frantically searched the store to no avail.

"The mirror on the counter. It's like something out of *Frozen*." Midnight dropped to the floor and retrieved CARA. Her heart pounded like a ticking clock. If she didn't release the spectral energy before the forensic team arrived, more people would end up in the hospital.

"Okay, I don't want to freak you out," Tabitha's voice shook as she glanced toward the front window. "But I think the policemen have finally finished talking to the woman. Let me know when it's done so I can take a photograph of the mirror in case there's another face."

"No, it's too dangerous. You have to stay behind me." Midnight dragged her gaze away from the mirror and back to the icy flames that only she could see. Tabitha looked like she wanted to protest but finally nodded.

"I will."

"Thank you." Midnight braced her knees and pressed her finger down on the trigger. A wave of white light burst out of CARA and hurtled toward the mirror. Sweat beaded on Midnight's brow as she waited for the white light to smother the strange blue flames. Instead, the white light turned to ice, like a frozen pillar suspended in the air.

"What's happening?" Tabitha whispered, but Midnight didn't answer. She pressed down on the trigger again. CARA shuddered in response before a second burst of white light poured out, pushing the frozen icicle back toward the mirror.

Midnight's muscles screamed in protest but she refused to stop, and finally the icy flames disappeared. For a second, a face flashed in the mirror before it fell with a thud to the ground.

"Please tell me it's over." Tabitha croaked as Midnight lowered CARA back to the floor.

She scanned the store, but all the spectral energy had definitely gone. Now they could see a display cabinet filled with gold and silver jewelry, with a blank spot where one pair of earrings had been.

All this for a lousy pair of earrings?

Suddenly Midnight was angry at the unknown thief. Their crimes were hurting people, and they didn't even seem to care.

"It's definitely over," she said just as there was a commotion outside. Both girls dropped to the floor and crawled behind one of the counters as the door swung open. Midnight's heart pounded as a couple of men in suits walked in, carrying large briefcases. The forensic team.

The two men walked straight to the cabinet where the missing earrings were, and where—up until a minute ago—the deadly mirror had been sitting. Tabitha tapped Midnight's shoulder and nodded toward the door, which was still open.

The longer they stayed in the store, the more chance there was of being caught. Tabitha signaled her agreement, and the pair of them inched their way to the door. Midnight peered out first, relieved that the policemen were still all deep in conversation with the red-faced woman.

Thunder cracked the sky, causing the police to all look up, and Midnight and Tabitha pulled their hoods up and ran down the street as quickly as they could.

That had been way too close.

CHAPTER SEVENTEEN

"See, this is why I *loathe* solving crimes," Tabitha groaned on Saturday afternoon as they huddled around a newspaper at the back of the local library. It was a lot less noisy than the school library, and there was no Mrs. Crown to give them the stink eye. "I mean, going to the jewelry store and containing the trapped spectral energy? That stuff is easy."

"Easy?" Midnight blinked, trying not to think about what had happened yesterday. They could've been arrested, or someone might have been seriously injured.

"Okay, not easy. But at least we know what to do," Tabitha corrected herself. "The same with local history.

It's like following a golden thread. Sometimes it might break, but you can always pick it up again. But with this, there's no thread."

"Preach." Midnight leaned her chair back before remembering that librarians frowned on chair leaning. She quickly brought the chair's legs back to the floor and drummed the table with her fingers instead. Tabitha was right. Nothing made sense.

They had two silver buttons.

Three crime scenes.

Two instances of pink fog.

A villain who shopped in department stores and liked pizza.

Terrible weather.

And it all added up to nothing.

She stared at the report. The news about yesterday's robbery had confirmed that the only thing taken was a pair of diamond earrings worth eighty thousand dollars. A gold nugget, two daggers, and now some earrings?

Who was this person?

"And in another dead end, I've been going over the list of people who work at the country club—not just the bellhops—and I can't link anyone to the museum or the jewelry store," Tabitha said.

"Do I even want to know *how* you got a list of everyone who works there?" Midnight ran a hand through her hair. This was like trying to do a jigsaw puzzle without knowing what the picture looked like.

"Trust me, it wasn't easy." Tabitha gave her a pained look. "It involved a phone call to Chloe, who asked her mom. And you know what's even worse? My mom was so happy I called Chloe that we're all going back to the country club for dinner. Tonight."

"I'll raise you dinner at the country club with learning how to dance like a Viking," Midnight said in a gloomy voice as she looked at her watch. "And speaking of that, I should go. I've missed so many things, and my mom's totally freaking out. Not helped by Taylor. The last thing I want to do is be late."

"Yeah, me too." Tabitha packed away her things and glanced at her cell phone. "My mom's waiting out front for me. We will figure this out."

"Of course," Midnight said, shuddering at the memory of the blazing wall at the country club. "And be careful tonight. Make sure you have your ghost app on."

"I will," Tabitha said before disappearing with a wave. Once she was gone, Midnight packed up her own work and made her way to the library foyer.

The floor was covered in tiny tiles, and on the ceiling was a mural of the Berry founding fathers. There were three sets of old-fashioned glass doors that all led out to the wide concrete stairs.

What a surprise. It was still raining. Midnight took one look at the gunmetal sky and texted her mom to ask for a ride. Her mom quickly replied that she'd be there in five minutes. Midnight walked over to one of the chairs scattered around the foyer and sat down. She was about to go over her notes again when something flickered in the corner of her eye. She blinked as a tiny fleck of spectral energy drifted past her. And another.

She looked around the foyer in awe as hundreds of the snowflake-like particles danced lazily through the air. Her face softened, and she stretched out her arm.

The tiny fragments darted around her wrist. Midnight had been so busy worrying about releasing the trapped spectral energy and trying to prevent it from being misused that she'd almost forgotten how beautiful it could be in its natural state.

She lifted up her other arm as it flickered with colors. Pearl, pink, pale blue, yellow. A shimmering rainbow of goodness. And someone was hurting it. Causing it to become something it wasn't.

"Hey, Midnight."

Logan?

Midnight dropped her arms to her sides and the spectral energy darted off, as if feeling the panic radiating from her.

Logan was wearing another Sherlock hoodie, and his dark eyes were bright with curiosity. She gulped, suddenly glad that Tabitha had convinced her to start wearing nicer clothes. After what had happened with Sav and Lucy, Midnight had almost been too scared to let herself enjoy picking out clothes. But now she was starting to reclaim her identity.

She glanced down at her blue-and-white-striped jeans and favorite apple-green jean jacket. Sav and Lucy would hate the color clash, but it made Midnight smile.

"Hey," she said when Logan reached her. "What are you doing here on a Saturday?"

"Just getting a few books to read. Mrs. Crown refuses to let me take more than three at a time," he said as he nodded to the large book bag hanging from his shoulder. "I haven't seen you around much at school."

"I've been kind of busy," she said, not bothering to mention that she'd been avoiding him. "Just with my mom's wedding and everything."

"Oh yeah. It's going to be a Viking thing. That's so cool."

"Not if you have to wear one of the outfits," Midnight said in a light voice. "Plus, tonight I have to learn to dance like a Viking. And before you ask…no, I don't have a clue what that means."

"Well, I'm sure you'll be great at it," he said, giving her a shy smile. "So, did you hear there was another robbery yesterday?"

She slowly nodded her head. "Yeah. At the jewelry store."

"Crazy, right?" he said before frowning. "But you know what I think is the weirdest part about it? All the rain and earthquakes only started when the robberies did."

"A-are you sure?" Midnight forced herself to stay calm, while she frantically crossed her fingers. The fact that Logan had made the connection proved two things. One, that he was brilliant. And two, that if she spent any more time with him, she might accidentally blurt out the truth and get kicked out of ASP for good.

"Yeah, I've even been correlating old weather reports," he said as he pulled out his cell phone. "Do you want to see?"

"Er, sure." She forced herself to stay calm as he held it up. It was impossible not to admire his style. "Wow. That's pretty crazy. So, what do you think it means?"

He gave a rueful smile, making him look cuter than ever. "That's the part I don't get. I mean, I know that they *can't* be connected, yet I can't stop thinking about it. Still, I guess I'll eventually figure it out."

Midnight sighed. *If only.* She and Tabitha knew loads more about the case than he did, and they hadn't even come close.

"Logan, this is going to sound weird. But when you're working on a case and you can't find any clues, no matter how hard you try, what do you do?"

"Well, that's easy," he said as he put his cell phone back in his jacket and they resumed walking. "I stop thinking about it and let it come to me. You'd be amazed how often the answer is actually sitting right under my nose."

"Thanks," she said as her mom's car pulled up outside the library. Midnight got to her feet and struggled into her raincoat, flipping her hood to stop the ever-present rain from soaking her.

"You're welcome. And have fun tonight. I bet you'll make the cutest Viking ever," he said as he waved goodbye to her. Despite everything that was going on, Midnight couldn't help but smile.

CHAPTER EIGHTEEN

"You should've invited Logan." Her mom adjusted Midnight's helmet. Her neck was already starting to ache from the weight. But at the mention of Logan's name, heat prickled Midnight's cheeks. Slim chance she'd let Logan see her wearing a shield maiden dress while holding hands with a bunch of Vikings doing the equivalent of "Ring around the Rosie."

"It's okay." Midnight peered around the room.

The Berry Community Hall had been transformed, and everywhere Midnight looked, there were long wooden oars hanging from the walls, along with animal skulls, fur rugs, and large pots covered in fine leather. Midnight had no idea if they were for cooking or for making music. Or both.

Her mom had said that after the dancing, the Sons of a Gunnar would be doing a Viking fight reenactment. But that was still an hour off, and the band—that consisted of flutes, weird lyres, and even weirder-looking bagpipes—was taking a break.

Outside, the rain thundered on, pounding against the steel roof. Her mom flinched. "I don't think this weather is ever going to get better. I can't help but think it's a sign."

A wave of guilt washed over Midnight. It wasn't a sign. It was just a terrible person doing terrible things. Terrible things that she hadn't been able to stop.

"Mom. No. You love Phil, and you were the one who told me that we all had to compromise. So perhaps this is how you compromise. If the rain doesn't stop, you could always have your wedding in here. I know it's not the side of a hill in a sea of spring flowers, but we could still buy loads of daffodils. I'm sure it would look amazing."

Her mom, who was wearing a full-length purple gown

with heavy leather armor over the top, suddenly dragged Midnight into a fierce hug. "Thank you, honey. I needed to hear that."

"It's going to be okay," Midnight promised just as Jerry walked over, closely followed by Ruth, who was almost unrecognizable with her dark hair in braids and her body covered in chain mail.

"Maggie, thank you so much for inviting me," Ruth said as Midnight's mom hugged her.

"You're welcome. Phil and I are so pleased you could come."

Ruth grinned and looked at Jerry. "Me too. To think that last week I was almost going to join the croquet club in the hope of meeting people."

"Croquet club?" Jerry looked outraged as he slipped an arm around Ruth's waist. "You would've hated it. Vikings are so much more fun."

"I'll say," Ruth said before seeming to remember that Midnight and her mom were standing there. "Anyway, I'm pleased to be here. And Midnight, you look so adorable in your costume."

"Er, thanks."

"That's what I keep trying to tell her, Ruth," Midnight's mom beamed with pride. "Still, at least she's wearing it. My other daughter, Taylor, has a gorgeous beet-dyed dress but two weeks ago suddenly refused to put it on."

"I'm sure she'll come around," Ruth said in a warm voice. "I remember being the same when I was that age. Especially since she has a boyfriend."

"Yes, fancy that she's dating my boss's son." Jerry looked over to where Taylor and Dylan were huddled in the corner, having an intense conversation.

Midnight stiffened. "Dylan's father works at the museum? I didn't know that."

"From what I can gather, Dylan and his dad have a bit of a strained relationship at the moment. I think they have different views on college. You probably met him when you did the class trip. Alan Staunton."

"Alan's his father?" Midnight blinked, recalling the smiling museum director. There wasn't much resemblance.

"That's right," Midnight's mom confirmed. "I thought you knew. Now I feel bad that I didn't tell you. Perhaps it would've helped with your article."

Not to mention solving an unsolvable crime. "Perhaps," Midnight agreed, her mind racing.

"Speaking of your article, how's it going?" Ruth asked, her eyes dancing with curiosity.

"Oh, um…it's going well. Almost finished." Midnight made a mental note to actually write one when this was finally over.

"Wonderful. You must bring around a copy for Elsie. And for me. After all, if it wasn't for your article, I might never have reconnected with Jerry." Ruth once again looked at Jerry like she'd just won the lottery. Midnight decided it was a good time to slip away.

She scanned the room to try to find Dylan. To the left, the band was returning to their instruments. She cringed. The first set they'd played had sounded more like a construction site than music. She had the feeling that Vikings made better warriors than composers.

Taylor was sitting by herself at one of the tables in far corner of the hall. Midnight hurried over, just as the low drone of the untuned pipe filtered out through the hall.

"Hey, Taylor. Where's Dylan?" Midnight asked, hoping to keep her voice casual.

"He had to go. Not that I can blame him," Taylor's mouth was pursed together in annoyance. "I mean, is this not the lamest thing in history?"

"Well, yeah," Midnight said. "It's Viking dancing. Of course it's lame, but it's for mom's wedding. Besides, it's not like you're wearing a costume. You should be grateful."

"I'd be more grateful if she'd let me go to the party tomorrow night," Taylor snapped before seeming to catch herself. As if realizing that it wasn't like Midnight could fix anything. "Anyway, I don't want to talk about it. Where's your partner in crime tonight? You two are normally joined at the hip."

"She had to go to the country club with her parents."

"Ugh. I hate that place. Dylan says when he used to work there, the staff weren't even allowed to keep their tips."

Midnight's mouth went dry. "Dylan worked at the country club? Since when?"

"He was a bellhop, but he quit three months ago. Why are you so interested?"

"No reason." Midnight tried to sound calm.

If he quit three months ago, that explained why he hadn't been on the list of employees that they'd studied.

Her head began to spin as the pipe player was joined by a roaring wail of guitar strings competing to be overheard. Dylan had means and opportunity for at least two of the crimes. And while she didn't know if he had a motive, the rest was too much of a coincidence to ignore.

"No reason. Taylor, do you have a photograph of Dylan on your cell phone?"

"Has anyone told you that you're weird?" Taylor snapped before letting out a disgruntled sigh and flicking through her photo album. "Fine. Here you go."

"Thanks," Midnight looked at the first photograph. However, there were so many filters on it that it was impossible to see for certain if the black smudge was there. And she had no way of knowing how long ago it was taken. She swiped the screen, but the next photo was just as bad. Dylan with rainbows tattoos on his face. She swiped again. Dylan with a donkey nose.

She was about to ask Taylor for an untouched one when her mom walked toward them. Taylor immediately turned her shoulder and stared in the other direction. Their mom let out a soft sigh.

"I've just come to remind you both to say hello to Phil's uncle. He's traveled from California to be here. He's actually a lovely man. He even agreed to be in yesterday's vlog. It's already had one hundred likes."

"Sure." Midnight nodded while Taylor made a grunting noise. Not that Midnight cared. All that mattered was trying to get a photograph of Dylan.

She stiffened.

Her mom had reshot yesterday's clip because the footage had been ruined. The footage that Taylor and Dylan had been in.

"M-mom, do you still have the ruined footage on your phone?" Midnight asked urgently.

"No, I was filming with Phil's camera." Her mom shook her head, then stopped. "Though I did set up my own phone to see if we could get some fun outtakes. Why?"

Trust me, you don't want to know.

"Er, I just wanted to see it," Midnight said, trying to keep her voice calm as her mom extracted her phone from the depths of her Viking costume and flicked from screen to screen before finally nodding.

"Yes, here it is."

"Thanks." Midnight took the phone and studied the clip. At first, it was only her mom on the screen—her blond curls sitting like a halo around her face—as she talked about what ingredients she was using. Then the camera finally panned out to include Taylor and Dylan.

Well, Midnight could only assume it was Dylan, because his entire face was covered by a black smudge. Planodiume.

Logan was right. The answer had been under her nose the entire time.

Taylor finally turned around and gave them an icy glare. "Oh God. I thought you were going to delete this thing. I mean, look at Dylan. He's totally covered by a black smudge. I swear she's only keeping it to embarrass me."

Actually, the fact that she'd kept it probably had saved Taylor's life.

"I have to make a call." Midnight handed the phone back and tried to keep her hands from shaking.

"Of course you do." Taylor folded her arms. "Don't mind me. I'm a virtual prisoner."

But Midnight didn't bother to answer as she hurried outside so that she could call Tabitha without being overheard. Finally, they had the breakthrough they were looking for. But the fact that the villain was her sister's boyfriend made it hard to feel happy. Still, the main thing that mattered was that it would soon be over and her life could return to normal.

CHAPTER NINETEEN

The wind howled down the street, sending eddies of leaves and rain flying in all directions. Next to her, Tabitha nervously shifted from foot to foot. Not that Midnight could blame her. The last time they'd snuck into a house, they'd almost been killed. It didn't exactly bring back great memories. But, after speaking to Peter Gallagher on the phone last night, it had been decided that the best thing to do was find the particle realigner and deactivate it before Dylan could use it again. Especially since the measurements Midnight had collected had shown the Black Stream was almost at its breaking point.

Another gust of rain blew against them as they waited for Dylan's mom to climb into her bright-yellow car and drive away.

"Finally." Tabitha lowered her umbrella and stepped out from behind the tree. They'd been there for half an hour and had watched Dylan drive out, closely followed by his father. And now that his mom had gone, the house would be empty.

"Let's just hope they're like every other family in America and have a spare key hidden under the door-mat." Midnight checked no one was looking. At least that was one thing the violent weather was good for. After she was satisfied, they jogged across the street and slipped around the side of the house to the back door.

"My heart's pounding," Tabitha admitted as she reached under the mat and then triumphantly held up a key. "And looks like you were right."

The only thing scarier than sneaking into the house was the idea of Dylan using the particle realigner again. Midnight gulped as they carefully shrugged out of their wet jackets and turned the key in the lock.

With a burst of resolve, she pushed open the door and

they stepped inside.

The house was modern and neat, with the kitchen and living area on the ground floor. A cat sleeping on a nearby chair looked up at them with interest before closing its eyes. Dylan had once mentioned his basement bedroom, so they quickly searched for the way down. It was just off the laundry room, and the stairs creaked as they descended.

The light flickered, and the cool air made Midnight's skin pucker as they reached the bottom. The room was a mess, with dirty laundry scattered all over the floor, while the wall was covered with writing. One word scribbled over and over: *Dominus*.

"Okay, creepy much?" Tabitha shuddered. "What does 'dominus' mean?"

"I don't know," Midnight whispered as an all-too-familiar buzzing noise hit her ears. "But there's something very wrong. There's spectral energy here. I can feel it and hear it, but why can't I see it?"

"Welcome to my world," Tabitha said before frowning. "And why didn't our ghost apps go off?"

"I don't know—"

A finger of spectral energy burst out of the wall.

Midnight jumped in shock. Since when did spectral energy do that?

The energy slithered to the ceiling before suddenly transforming into a dagger. It hung in the air, rocking from side to side before flying toward them.

The buzzing in her ears increased to a high-pitched screech.

Midnight grabbed Tabitha's arm and pulled her out of the way as the energy dagger struck the far wall, then clattered to the ground.

"W-what just happened?" Tabitha's face drained of color. "I could feel something brush past me. Almost like it was cutting my skin."

"I don't know." Midnight jumped to the left as another dagger swayed from side to side and then came hurtling at them. The air whistled as it flew past. "This spectral energy is…different. It's like a weapon. *Duck!*" she yelled as a third dagger flew toward them. They both fell to the floor.

"We have to get out of here." Tabitha panted, wildly looking around despite the fact she couldn't see anything. "He's created some kind of booby trap."

"It also explains the daggers that were stolen. Somehow he's managed to combine them with spectral energy," Midnight said as another black, misty dagger appeared. It swayed side to side before slicing through the air so fast it was difficult to see. She reached for a nearby baseball bat and managed to knock it to one side.

Then she let out a strangled gasp as hundreds of inky-black daggers shimmered into life, all cast from spectral energy. The buzzing in her ear increased and the temperature dropped, turning their breath to steam.

"Don't freak out, but you need to start crawling for the stairs. Right now," Midnight yelled as the daggers began to slowly sway.

"Okay." Tabitha scrambled to the stairs as Midnight followed, holding the baseball bat high in the air. One dagger launched itself at them, and Midnight swatted it away. Then another one.

Her heart pounded as Tabitha reached the staircase, Midnight right behind her. Another dagger came toward them. She tried to swat it, but it nicked her skin and ice-cold pain ran up her arm. The room went deathly silent. All the daggers were swaying from side to side.

"Tabitha. Stand up and go as fast as you can. Do it now," Midnight said. Tabitha didn't bother to reply. Instead she raced up the stairs. Midnight followed her, taking the stairs two at a time until they reached the top. They slammed the door shut just in time to hear the thud of the daggers pounding into the wood.

By silent agreement they ran from the kitchen, quickly locking the door behind them and grabbing their raincoats. They didn't even dare to look at each other until they were back in the safety of Midnight's bedroom.

"We need to call Peter Gallagher right now," Tabitha said grimly. "Because whatever that was, I don't want to have to go through it again."

That would make two of them. Midnight reached for her phone and tried not to notice that her hands were still shaking.

CHAPTER TWENTY

"*Dominus* means 'master' in Latin," Peter Gallagher said in a tight voice. For once, he'd answered his phone on the second ring, listening in silence as Midnight tried to explain what had just happened. "Which means somehow he's managed to bind the planodiume from the Black Stream to his will."

"Like a weapon?" Midnight whispered.

"That's right. It would seem that the more he's used the weapon, the more he's managed to harness and control the planodiume, despite the ruptures. The flames that burned the security guard at the country club. The ice surrounding the jewelry store. But this final attack…" He paused, as if remembering that it was a bad idea to freak out the twelve-year-old spectral protector. Well, too late for that.

"So, what happens now?" Midnight gulped.

"We'll be there in eighteen hours. In the meantime, you're not to approach Dylan Staunton or try to retrieve the particle realigner. This is a Code Black," he said as the line started to break up.

Midnight flinched, remembering page ninety-three of the manual:

> Code Black is only issued in the direst situations. When there is a high likelihood of civilian or protector death. It is vital that only highly trained personnel deal with such situations.

"What about Taylor? I'll need to tell her something, just to make sure she doesn't go near him."

"Absolutely not. I know it's difficult, but remember the rules. Unvetted civilians can make a dangerous situation worse. Keep her away from him, but don't, under any circumstances, tell her why."

"Easier said than done," Midnight said, but the crackling got worse and then the call disconnected. Midnight put her cell phone down and turned to Tabitha, who was sitting cross-legged on Midnight's bed. Her black skirt was fanned out around her, and her face was pale.

"I take it the call went dead."

A Code Black meant that it might not just be the call that ended up dead. Midnight swallowed, her stomach tight with nerves. How was she going to last for eighteen hours until the ASP team arrived?

The only good news was that her mom still refused to budge on Taylor going to the party, which meant as soon as they'd returned from their trip to the market, Taylor had stormed into her room and hadn't come out since.

"I still can't believe that your sister's boyfriend is the villain. I mean, he's only eighteen, and according to our research, his family has always given him everything he wanted." Tabitha flipped open her MacBook and looked at the spreadsheet they'd spent the previous night compiling. Along with Dylan's connection to the museum and country club, he'd also had a part-time job at the jewelry store before getting fired for being rude to a customer. Tabitha had stopped to see Elsie Perkins earlier in the morning and shown the old woman a photograph. Elsie had confirmed that Dylan was the one who'd gone into the attic.

It also explained why there'd been planodiume ruptures in the headphone section of the department store, and Midnight had since discovered the pizza parlor was where Dylan and Taylor often went. As for why he'd stolen earrings, all Midnight could guess was that they were a present for Taylor.

Her worry increased.

"Apart from paying for his gap year." Midnight said as a sound came from the hallway. She raced out just as Taylor emerged from her bedroom. Her long, blond hair was pushed over one ear, and she was wearing a jacket, as if she was planning to go out.

Not good.

"Hey," Midnight said, trying to ignore the stink eye her sister was giving her.

"What do you want?" Taylor snapped. Her mood obviously hadn't improved from yesterday.

"N-nothing." Midnight shook her head as Tabitha joined her at her door.

"Hey, Taylor. Cute jacket. Are you going out?" Tabitha asked with a surprising amount of finesse. Her friend had definitely improved her interpersonal skills.

"Not that it's any of your business, but I'm going to Donna's house." Taylor swung toward the staircase. Midnight and Tabitha followed her.

"Are you sure that's a good idea? The rain's still pretty heavy," Midnight said, which earned her a get-out-of-my-way look. At the same time, the ghost app went off, and Taylor took the opportunity to stalk out the back door without another word.

"Okay, how's this for a plan," Tabitha said as she reached for her coat, which she'd left on the hook by the doorway. "I'll follow her, ninja style, and wait outside Donna's house, while you go and dispose of the spectral energy."

The last thing Midnight wanted was to let her sister out of her sight. But short of telling Taylor what was going on, there wasn't much else she could do.

* * *

Midnight paused to wipe the rain out of her eyes as she climbed off the bus. It hadn't taken her long to reach the parking lot where some spectral energy had been trapped in the rearview mirror of a Toyota. She'd quickly released it and made the return trip.

CARA was a deadweight in her backpack, and the sky was bullet gray. Thunder rumbled all around her, closely followed by crackling bursts of lightning so bright that Midnight had to look away. Torrents of water ran down the sidewalk as she hurried toward Donna's house, where Tabitha was hunched miserably behind an oak tree across the road.

"Every now and then I catch a glimpse of her by the window," Tabitha said as Midnight handed her the cup of hot chocolate she'd picked up after she'd released the spectral energy. Another peel of thunder echoed around them, causing them both to jump. "The good news is I've downloaded a flight app so we can follow Peter Gallagher's progress."

"Excellent." Midnight looked at her friend's phone while Tabitha gratefully took a sip of the warm drink. Peter's flight was somewhere over Europe and still on track.

"Hey, Midnight, Tabitha. What are you guys doing here?" a voice asked, and Malie appeared before them. She had an oversize umbrella in one hand and leashes attached to two small dogs in her other. Gone were the colored cosplay dress and the tiara, and her awesome dark curly hair hung down around her shoulders. Droplets of rain clung to her jacket, and the two small dogs at her heels were covered in miniature raincoats.

"Um, Malie. Hey." Midnight's mind whirled as she tried to come up with a suitable explanation of why they were hiding behind a tree in the pouring rain. None was forthcoming.

"It's a long story," Tabitha said with an intimidating shrug before her gaze honed in on the two small dogs. "I didn't know you had dogs."

"I don't." Malie shook her head, and the dogs yelped. "They're Veronica and Mr. George. It's my new business. I'm a dog walker. First one in Berry."

Midnight's mouth dropped open. "When I saw you at the mall that day, you said you were going to make a lot of money. Is that what you meant?"

"Well, yeah." Malie nodded. "I had already started

handing out flyers, so I knew it wouldn't take long. Why? What did you think I meant?"

"Nothing." Midnight quickly shook her head, not wanting to admit the truth. "I'm glad it's working out for you."

"Thanks," Malie said as the two dogs began to protest at standing still for so long. "Okay, that's my cue to go, but I just wanted to say sorry for being so mean to you both. I'm pretty embarrassed. I'm not spending time with Sav and Lucy anymore. Well, I should say they're not spending time with me anymore. I took your advice and acted like myself. It didn't go down too well."

"It's their loss," Midnight said in a fierce voice, though Tabitha was still eyeing Malie with a frosty gaze. "Life's so much easier when you're hanging out with people who actually understand you."

"Yeah, I'm starting to get that," Malie said before giving Tabitha—who was still scowling—a shy smile. "And I'm really sorry I ignored you in the library when I first started at the school. I was worried that you might think I was a dork for researching my mom's family tree. Plus, Sav and Lucy had warned me against you both."

Tabitha's animosity unfurled. "One, I don't judge. And two, if I did judge, I would've been impressed. I might've even helped you."

Malie nodded. "Tyson said that. He sits next to me in math, and when he saw I had a map of the cemetery, he suggested I talk to you because you are smart and awesome."

"He really said that?"

"Totally." Malie nodded, her wild curls bouncing around her shoulders. "So he decided to ask you himself. I think the fact he had a reason helped give him courage."

"I'm not that scary," Tabitha muttered, in contrast to the smile on her face. Then she wrinkled her brow. "What were you hoping to find out? Tyson only talked to me about the Irongate mausoleum. I can't see how your mom could be related to them, because I've studied their family tree in depth."

"We're not," Malie said. "I've been trying to track down my mom's long-lost great-uncle. His name was Reginald Ironguard, but he'd been using another last name. I saw Irongate and was grasping at straws. Apparently, he lived here in the seventies, but we haven't been able to track him since he went to the Vietnam War. My mom's an orphan, and I wanted to give her something. That probably sounds stupid."

"Not at all," Midnight said before letting out a gasp as she turned to Tabitha. "You don't think Reginald is Reggie, do you?"

Tabitha's eyes sparkled as she reached for her phone. "I've got no idea, but I'll definitely find out." Several moments later she looked up. "I'm sorry, but I think the guy you're looking for is Reginald Stephen Ireland who died in Vietnam. But Midnight and I know someone who'd love to meet you and your family, and she'd be more than happy to tell you all about him."

"Really?" Malie's large brown eyes filled with tears. "You don't know what this will mean to my mom. Thank you both so much. I guess this has taught me once and for all that I really need to listen to my instincts and not worry so much about what everyone else thinks."

"The good thing about learning the hard way is that you don't tend to forget it." Tabitha gave her a rare smile as the dogs started to bark again. Malie wrinkled her nose and tightened her grip on the umbrella.

"Okay, I really have to go now. But I'll see you both at school tomorrow?"

"You sure will," Midnight said as they watched Malie and the dogs jog away. Tabitha's eyes were still shining, though it was hard to tell if it was because she'd just solved a local history riddle or because Tyson Carl really did like her. Either way, it was nice to see her friend happy. But before she could say anything, Donna's front door opened and Taylor stepped out. A flash of lightning burst through the sky, clearly showing Midnight's sister's face.

All thoughts of Malie disappeared as they waited until Taylor reached the end of the street before they stepped out from behind the oak tree. They carefully followed her three blocks, and it wasn't until Midnight's house came into view that she allowed herself to let out her breath. If Taylor had decided to meet Dylan, she wasn't sure what they would've done. Instead, they watched her walk through the back door. They waited until the light in her upstairs bedroom went on and headed in.

"Not you too?" Midnight's mom said with a frown, taking in their drenched clothing. "Honestly, I don't know what's gotten into you all today."

"Er, it was a hot chocolate emergency," Midnight said as she pointed to Tabitha's cup.

"That's right." Tabitha nodded her head in agreement, sending a splatter of water out around the kitchen. Midnight's mom just shrugged.

"Well, you'd better both go upstairs and get dry. And like I've just told your sister, with the way the weather is going, I think you should stay in for the rest of the day or get me to drive you. Okay?"

As long as Taylor stayed in, Midnight would too.

"Sure." She nodded as they hurried up the stairs. Music blared from Taylor's room, and she could hear her sister speaking on the phone. She didn't sound happy, but then again, lately she never did. And right now all that mattered was that she was safe.

It didn't take them long to get into dry clothes, and they then settled down to stare at the flight app. As the plane passed over Europe and began to cross the Atlantic, some of the tightness in Midnight's stomach decreased. It was five in the afternoon, which meant in seven hours ASP would arrive, and it would all be over.

Peter Gallagher and his team would swoop in and fix everything.

Dylan would be caught and given the antidote.

The particle realigner would be confiscated and taken into safekeeping. Life would return to normal. Her spreadsheets would no longer be blurred and confusing. It would—

"Midnight." Her mom burst through the door, her face lined with worry. "Have you seen your sister?"

Midnight jumped to her feet, her brow wrinkled. "What do you mean? She's in her bedroom. She's been there all afternoon."

"No, she's not." Her mom's eyes filled with horror. "And her Vespa's gone. I've just called Dylan's parents, but he's not at home. They said he'd been acting out lately—refusing to speak to them because they wouldn't fund his gap year. I can't believe she's really disobeyed me and gone to that party."

"What?" The blood drained from Midnight's face as she hurried to her sister's room and flung open the door. But her mom was right. The room was empty. Taylor really had gone.

CHAPTER TWENTY-ONE

"Are you sure you don't mind staying here?" Midnight's mom asked, deep lines etched into her face as she stood at the door. Phil was already in the car, setting the GPS for their journey. The sky was inky black, and trees were bent sideways with the wind.

"I'm sure," Midnight assured her. Her mom had already called the party, and there was no sign of her sister and Dylan. But since the police refused to register it as a missing person's complaint until Taylor had been gone for twenty-four hours, her mom and Phil had decided to make the one-hour drive. Their main worry was that if they did find Taylor and Dylan, there wouldn't be room in the car for everyone.

Midnight had reluctantly agreed to stay at home.

Besides, what if Taylor wasn't there?

What if she was still somewhere in Berry? With Dylan. The crazy guy who was pumped up with planodiume and capable of anything? Midnight bit her lip. The only thing stopping her from confessing everything was the worry her mom wouldn't believe it, and that would make Midnight's chance of saving Taylor even more difficult.

"We're going to find her," Tabitha said in a low voice as soon as the taillights disappeared from sight. "I was thinking. What if we look for some different ghost apps. Something that could pick up high levels of spectral energy…like a metal detector. Then we can cover more ground."

"Okay," Midnight managed to answer, guilt eating at her stomach. They hurried back into the house and packed everything they might need before heading out. ASP had given her plenty of expense money, so Midnight booked a taxi while Tabitha downloaded an array of electromagnetic apps in hope of picking up any trace of Dylan.

They'd also made a list of possible places where her sister and her crazy boyfriend might be. No stone left unturned.

Their ride turned up ten minutes later.

Doris was a nice lady who chatted about knitting as she took them from location to location. She was happy to wait at each spot as Midnight and Tabitha climbed out, desperately searching for any sign of Taylor. But by seven o'clock that night, Midnight was starting to panic. They'd visited all of Taylor's friends and favorite places, and they still hadn't even had a whiff.

Where was she?

Her mom had sent a frantic text, letting Midnight know that they'd arrived at the party and Taylor wasn't there. They were going to drive around the area, stopping everywhere they could, and could Midnight stay with Tabitha for the night? Even Phil had started texting, telling her that he was sure everything would be okay.

But what if it wasn't?

Midnight called her sister's number for the zillionth time but just got the same message. *It's Taylor. Leave a message. Or, whatever.*

Her stomach churned as they passed the pizza parlor on Winchester Road—the one Dylan and her sister went to on a regular basis. It was a long shot, but right now it was better than no shot.

"Doris, would you mind dropping us off here?"

"Of course not, doll." Doris pulled to a stop, and Midnight thrust a handful of money at her. She didn't even wait for a receipt, despite the fact it was in the rulebook. Right now, all she cared about was finding her sister.

Midnight once again hoisted her backpack onto her shoulders. CARA seemed to be getting heavier by the minute. Tabitha was right behind her as they walked into the restaurant. Despite the black rain-soaked sky, the place was warm and filled with the heady scent of cheese, flour, and spices. Midnight scanned the restaurant as a server came over.

"I was hoping you could help me. I'm looking for my sister, Taylor Reynolds." Midnight held up her phone for the server to see. It wasn't her sister's best shot, which ironically was why Midnight had it on her phone. Just to annoy Taylor. She swallowed hard to stop from losing it.

"Sorry." The server shook her head and led them to a table. Midnight was about to protest, but Tabitha held back her arm.

"We need to take a break and regroup," Tabitha said as they both slid into the booth. Midnight silently nodded as numbness crept into her skin while Tabitha ordered a couple of drinks and some garlic bread. Midnight checked the flight app again, hoping the small plane icon would've magically reached its destination ahead of time. But it hadn't. Peter Gallagher and the team were still several hours away.

"What's wrong?" Tabitha said, sensing the panic, and when Midnight held up the screen, her friend winced. "Oh."

Yeah, oh.

"Hey, we're going to find her," Tabitha repeated yet again.

"What if we don't?" Midnight finally allowed herself to say the words out loud. They caught in her throat, and the room began to spin. "What if he hurts her?"

Tabitha was silent. Midnight didn't need to be psychic to know she was thinking about the flying daggers that had attacked them in Dylan's basement. It was hard enough to dodge them with full vision. But Taylor wouldn't be able to see the full spectral energy. And she'd be scared. Confused.

"He won't," Tabitha said, but it was without conviction.

"He might. All because I didn't tell her who he was. This is all my fault."

"No, it's Dylan's fault for being an overprivileged kid who turned to the dark side just because he didn't get his way," Tabitha said in a firm voice. "But, Midnight, we can't give up. Imagine if we'd given up when Miss Appleby was about to leave town. You saved thousands of trapped souls by stopping her. And you'll stop this too."

"How? We've searched everywhere." The words were like dust in her mouth as the server brought over their order. Midnight's phone beeped and she snatched at it, hoping it was from Taylor.

Instead it was from Malie and was a photograph of one of the dogs clutching the cosplay dress in its jaws. The caption read, "Veronica agrees with you. It's much better to be myself."

Midnight pushed the phone away and stared at the beads of moisture trailing down her glass. If only her problem could be as simply solved. But she was already being herself. She was doing everything right. Everything she was meant to do, and look where it had gotten her. Her sister was in danger. For all Midnight knew…

She froze as she picked up her phone again and studied the photograph. There in the corner was a slither of pink fog.

Eliza?

What was the ghost of Eliza Irongate doing in Malie's photograph?

The first time she'd appeared had been when Midnight was at the movies with Logan. The second time was when she knocked over Midnight's overloaded spreadsheet. The one where she was desperately trying not to let the different parts of her life blur.

She let out a soft gasp.

"I know that look," Tabitha said. "What's going on? Did you have an idea of where she might be?"

"No, not a clue," Midnight said, but for the first time since Taylor had disappeared, some of the tension in her stomach lessened. "But I know someone who can help us. Someone who's much better at looking for clues than we are."

Tabitha's eyes widened in understanding. "Logan? But what about ASP? He's an unvetted civilian."

"Yes, and perhaps if I'd trusted my instincts and asked for his help sooner, none of this would be happening. You told me I couldn't compartmentalize my life, and I think that's what Eliza's been trying to tell me too." Midnight scrolled through her address book. Logan's number came up, along with a photo of him pulling a goofy face. She took a deep breath and hit Dial before she could change her mind.

"Midnight, hey. Is everything okay?" he said, answering on the third ring.

"Not exactly. I need some help, but it's kind of complicated."

"Complicated is my middle name," he said, his voice warm. Somehow she knew he was smiling. "So, what's going on…"

Chapter Twenty-Two

"No, you hold it the other way," Tabitha scolded half an hour later as they sat in Midnight's bedroom and showed Logan the weapons she used on a daily basis. After Midnight had explained everything, he'd agreed to meet them back at her house so they could come up with a plan.

He'd been waiting for them at her back door, his hair slicked back from the rain and his cheeks red, as if he'd run the five blocks to her house. Her heart pounded with gratitude that he'd agreed so readily, accepting what she'd told him as if it was the most normal thing in the world. As if *she* was normal.

"And you use this to release the spectral energy and stop it from turning into planodiume?" Logan double--checked as he continued to turn CARA over in his hands. Then he looked at Midnight and seemed to read her expression. He put CARA down and coughed. "Sorry. So, I've been thinking about your sister. I don't suppose you know her App Store log-in?"

"No." Midnight shook her head before suddenly getting to her feet. "But I do know where her diary is, and Dylan was telling her how old-school she was to write down her passwords. But even if I can find it, how will that help?"

"Because if she's anything like my older sister, she'll have a Find My Phone app on her account. And if we can get in and activate it, we could get the GPS location. Assuming she has her phone on her."

"It's permanently glued to her side." Midnight scrambled to her feet and raced into Taylor's bedroom. She paused on the threshold for a moment and looked around. Normally, stepping into her sister's room was punishable by a screaming fit of epic proportions. Midnight swallowed the thought down. If this worked, then Taylor would soon be home, and she could scream at Midnight as much as she wanted.

A pile of clothing was on the bed and another pile on the chest by the window, but Midnight was looking for an old suitcase. It had once belonged to their dad. Taylor pretended she only liked it because of the retro vibe, but Midnight suspected it was more than that. Which also explained why that's where she kept her journals.

She snapped back the clasps and grabbed the pink note-book with gold writing on the cover. She flipped through it to the last page, which was titled, "My Passwords. Midnight, if you're looking at this, you're dead."

Tears pricked at her eyes, but she wiped them away and hurried back to her room where Logan and Tabitha were hovering over his laptop.

"I got it." Midnight read out the password and user-name and waited as Logan entered them. They collectively held their breath as the browser ticked over before Taylor's account flashed on the screen.

Logan pressed his mouth together in concentration as his fingers flew across the keyboard, and then he smiled as a GPS map appeared on the screen.

"Okay. So, this was updated ten minutes ago, and it looks like Taylor's phone is at…at the cemetery."

"What?" Tabitha immediately leaned forward and increased the size before turning to them both. "It's plot eight-three. That's the Irongate mausoleum."

"Are you sure?" Logan asked.

"This is Tabitha. Of course she's sure." Midnight reached for her jacket and started to load her backpack with CARA. "We need to get there right now."

Tabitha's face was lined with worry. "Peter Gallagher isn't going to like this. And I don't mean because of Logan. He said it was a Code Black. What if there are more flying ghost daggers?"

"Flying ghost daggers?" Logan's eyes were like saucers. "Is that a thing?"

"Unfortunately, yes it is." Midnight stopped her packing and peeled back her sleeve. The welt from where the dagger had grazed her was still red and puckered. "Which is why you two should stay here. It's not fair for you to come when you can't even see what Dylan might be throwing at us."

"I think Tabitha meant that you shouldn't go either," Logan said in a soft voice, but Midnight shook her head.

"I don't care. Mom and Phil are still looking for Taylor at all the stops on the way to the party, and Peter Gallagher's two hours from landing. I don't have a choice."

"And no way am I letting you go alone," Tabitha said as she looked around the room, her eyes settling on Taylor's field hockey stick. She marched up and slung it over her shoulders. "I just meant that we should be careful."

"Actually, what we really need is armor," Logan said before catching sight of Midnight's Viking helmet. "I don't suppose your mom's fiancé has any of his Viking costumes here?"

Midnight and Tabitha both stopped and looked at him. Tabitha was the first to speak. "Of course. That's a brilliant idea. I've picked up that chain mail. It weighs a ton. If anything will stop ghost daggers, hopefully that will."

Midnight looked at both her friends and gave them a wobbly smile. "Thank you. Both of you, I seriously owe you. Big time."

"Let's save your sister, and then worry about that," Tabitha said as they finished packing and went down to the formal dining room currently being used as wedding headquarters. It was filled with costumes, large cooking vats, boxes of plates, an oversize boat oar. Everywhere Midnight looked were signs of a wedding. A wedding that would never happen if they couldn't save Taylor.

Midnight swallowed hard as she opened the large chest that contained some of Phil's collection. Fifteen minutes later, they were all wearing heavy steel helmets, oversize chain mail, and leather bands wrapped around their arms and legs.

"Okay," Midnight said, her armor creaking as she called a taxi. "Let's do this."

Chapter Twenty-Three

At the best of times, Berry Cemetery was a creepy place with crumbling tombstones that poked out of the ground like broken teeth, all overshadowed by long, sweeping branches that rustled from unseen wind.

At ten o'clock on a rainy Sunday night, it was worse. So much worse.

"Follow me." Tabitha led them through the cemetery gates. Thunder rumbled across the skies, followed by cracks of lightning bright enough to illuminate the shadowy surroundings. Wind howled all around them, but Midnight forced herself to follow Tabitha, who knew the place better than she knew her own house.

Logan was right behind them. He and Tabitha had spent the entire car ride over discussing the best way to stop Dylan from hurting anyone. But all Midnight could do was focus on her breathing.

The Irongate mausoleum was plain, with three concrete walls covered in trailing ivy. It was surrounded by a rusty fence and an old gate, which Tabitha pushed open.

Despite the pounding rain, they could see that the grass that had once grown there was dead, like the life had been sucked out of it. Dead plant life was never a good sign. It meant that planodiume was nearby.

Midnight gulped as she spotted light leaking out from under the mausoleum door.

She put down her backpack and lifted out CARA. Lightning once again split the sky, and CARA glowed against the darkness. Midnight had no idea if the weapon would work against Dylan, but she had to try. At least Taylor would know she wasn't alone.

The Viking armor chafed Midnight's skin, but after weeks of wearing it while her mom fitted her outfit, she was used to the weight and could move easily in it.

Behind her, Tabitha and Logan weren't quite as comfortable as they awkwardly moved.

The door creaked as they pushed it open to reveal a small, damp room. It was icy cold, lit only by a small camping lantern sitting on a concrete plinth. Midnight had a terrible feeling that underneath the plinth was the body of either George or William Irongate. She swallowed and continued her search. It almost appeared as though the room was empty before her torch landed on the figure of Dylan, leaning against one of the walls while holding a pair of daggers in his hand.

His face was a swirl of darkness, almost identical to the image Midnight had seen in the mirror that first day at the museum. There was a copper weapon by his feet. It was cone-shaped, with small tubes running around it. The particle realigner. Midnight shuddered.

"Oh, you ruined the surprise," he drawled as dark flicks of planodiume wrapped around his entire body like a tattoo. He tossed a dagger into the air and caught it before nodding to the other side of the room. "And yes, before you ask. She's here."

"Taylor?" Midnight swept the torch across the room.

Her sister was sitting in a chair, swirls of spectral energy wrapped around her ankles and wrists, keeping her prisoner.

"Midnight? Is that you? I can't get up. He's done something to trap me here. I don't understand. Dylan's gone crazy."

"You can say that again," Tabitha piped up as she waved her torch back to where Dylan was still standing. "His eyes are completely black."

"You can see that?" Midnight gasped, realizing just how much planodiume he must've been exposed to. Even Miss Appleby had managed to hide her true appearance from the world. He'd also written *dominus* all over the wall again.

Midnight gulped. That didn't bode well.

"Excuse me, Viking losers. In case you're forgetting, I'm the guy with the daggers. So, here's how this is going to work. You're going to put down that oversize Nerf gun and sit. Then Taylor's going to have a little attitude adjustment before we head off to Europe."

"And I told you that I'm not going anywhere with you," Taylor snarled, giving him one of her best glares. Midnight had to respect her sister's fighting spirit.

"You think you can buy me with stolen goods, but you're wrong."

"You see, here's the problem." Dylan's smile didn't reach his eyes. "Now that you know what I've been doing, I can't exactly let you leave. And since you won't come with me, there's only one thing I can do."

He raised his hands, and dark tendrils rose up from the ground like a fountain. Midnight sucked in her breath as he flicked his fingers and the spectral energy turned to daggers.

Dylan noted her reaction and quirked an eyebrow. "You can see them?"

"See what?" Taylor snarled at him. "Oh, and by the way, you're still crazy."

"And you're still stuck in the chair." Dylan growled before turning his attention back to Midnight. "I always thought you were a weird kid. This just proves it."

"*I'm* weird?" Midnight said, trying not to notice the way the daggers swayed from side to side. "Do you have any idea what you're doing? Where this power is coming from?"

"I'm so sick of people thinking that I'm stupid just because I don't want to go to college." Dylan's face turned into a dark mask. "Of course I know where it comes from. I've been researching planodiume for years, ever since I found out that Berry was surrounded by a Black Stream. But until I discovered William Irongate had actually found a weapon to harness it, I thought it was just theory. I guess I should thank dear old Dad for making me collect all that stupid stuff for the museum."

Midnight stared at him. He knew what spectral energy was. That he was using the souls of the dead. And he didn't even care.

She tightened her grip on CARA as the daggers inched forward. Her plan was to try to release the trapped energy. Her finger tightened on the brass button just as Dylan brought his hand down like a conductor performing a symphony.

Daggers flew through the air, and Midnight pressed down on CARA. A wall of white light shot out, trapping the daggers in a glowing shield of energy. The air hissed, and Dylan's smug expression fell away as sweat beaded up on Midnight's brow. Finally, the daggers disappeared, and tiny shards of pink spectral energy floated to the ceiling.

"So, it's not just a modified Nerf gun," Dylan mused before waving his hands again. The dark tendrils that had been wrapped around him raced up and dragged the floating pink spectral energy back toward him, like a fisherman throwing a net.

"No," she gasped.

"Yes." He grinned. Then he gave another flick of his wrist, and this time the tendrils re-formed as a giant beast. It was eight feet tall, almost touching the ceiling of the mausoleum. Its eyes glowed as the rest of its body dripped with darkness.

Midnight shrank back as the beast raised a large claw, deadly talons glittering against the flickering light as they slashed the air. She jumped just in time, before the beast turned its attention to where Tabitha and Logan were huddled.

"Run," Midnight shouted, sending her friends scattering just as the giant claw landed where they'd been standing moments ago. Panic lodged in her throat. She doubted the armor would stop the beast from hurting them.

"Is it bad?" Tabitha asked, holding the hockey stick high in the air.

"It's not ideal," Midnight admitted, almost pleased her friends couldn't see what she could. The beast howled and stormed toward the chair where Taylor was sitting.

No. Midnight hoisted CARA back up and pressed down on the lever. White energy hurtled around the bear, locking it in like an iceberg. Her hands shook as the creature finally dissolved.

"It's like you don't learn," Dylan drawled as he raised his hands, and once again the pale-pink energy darted to him. Midnight's mouth trembled as he re-formed it back into daggers. "But hey, we can play this game as long as you want to."

Hope leached from her.

Any thought of her holding on until ASP arrived was shattered. She probably wouldn't survive another round. She was spent. Suddenly, she understood why it was so dangerous to have unvetted civilians involved. After all, she could see what was happening and still couldn't stop it. But Tabitha, Logan, and Taylor were blind to it all.

She stared at the writing on the wall. *Dominus.* This was all because Dylan had managed to bind the spectral energy to him. They were all going to die because of one lousy word.

"What's going on?" Taylor screamed, her earlier bravado fading.

"Midnight's trying to stop your crazy boyfriend from killing us all," Tabitha snapped. But all Midnight could think was that she'd failed. Whatever power Dylan had over the spectral energy, it was stronger than what CARA could do. The weapon sagged in her hands.

"He's not my boyfriend." Taylor spat out as she glared at Dylan. "He's not who I thought he was. In fact, he's the opposite. And when this is over, I'm so updating my status. Because I have one word for you—"

"Liberate," Midnight suddenly said as an idea hit her. One word. Dylan had used just one word to create so much evil. *Dominus.* To dominate. Could she stop him just as easily?"

"Actually, I was going to say 'loser,'" Taylor snapped, but Midnight shook her head as she looked to Tabitha and Logan.

"Liberate. How do you say it in Latin?"

Tabitha's eyes widened as her fingers stabbed at her phone, but Logan beat her to it. "*Liberate*," he called out as he fumbled around in his pocket and produced a piece of chalk. He broke it in half, and he and Tabitha darted to different parts of the wall and began writing.

"It won't work," Dylan snapped, though some of his swagger had gone. "You think I just wrote the word without doing anything else? I had the power of the Black Stream to help me." As he spoke, he waved his hand, and more daggers appeared, aimed at where Midnight's friends were frantically writing.

"Yeah, and I have the power of the Afterglow to help me," Midnight said as she held up CARA once again. A burst of pink fog slid out from under the plinth. Eliza! Midnight slammed her finger on the lever and aimed as the daggers went hurtling toward Tabitha and Logan.

White energy wrapped around them like a blanket.

Dylan raised his other hand, but before he could do anything, a burst of emerald fog slammed into him, knocking him to the ground and trapping him there. Emerald fog? Midnight's mouth dropped open. The fog had come from George Irongate's coffin.

"Okay, someone seriously needs to tell me what's going on," Taylor said as the spectral energy that had been trapping her faded away. Her sister might not have been able to see it, but she could obviously feel it leaving and quickly stood up. But before Midnight could answer, the white energy raced out the door, followed closely by swirling pink-and-emerald fog.

Midnight looked at Dylan, who was knocked out in a crumpled heap of the floor. He wasn't going anywhere in a hurry.

She raced outside, closely followed by her friends and sister, and watched as George and Eliza's spirits burst through the white energy, causing a splintering eruption of light.

"Whoa!" Logan said, the lights reflecting in his shining eyes.

"It's beautiful," Tabitha said as a blaze of energy funneled up into the sky like a rainbow against the dark night. "And hey, it's stopped raining."

Midnight looked around. The sodden cemetery was now glittering as if it were filled with a thousand diamonds, and the air filled with the sound of night birds and insects, all venturing out now that the rain had finished.

"Okay, someone seriously needs to tell me what just happened." Taylor hugged her arms to her chest as footsteps approached.

"Yes, that's what I'd like to know," an English accent agreed, and they all turned around to see a middle-aged man dressed in an immaculate black suit walking toward them.

It was Peter Gallagher. Midnight's boss.

CHAPTER TWENTY-FOUR

"Okay, so on a scale of one to ten, how mad do you think he looks?" Midnight clutched the blanket closer to her chest. It had been half an hour since ASP had arrived, and after assessing what had happened, they'd drawn Taylor and Logan to one side for a debriefing. Midnight had the feeling that the word *unvetted* would be thrown around a lot.

Peter Gallagher had then commanded Midnight and Tabitha to stay where they were while the ASP team headed into the mausoleum, where they took all kinds of readings and measurements. They'd emerged five minutes ago and were still having an intense conversation.

"It's really hard to say. He has a major poker face," Tabitha said with just a hint of admiration in her voice. "But whatever happens, you know I'll support you. And if you want to quit ASP, then I promise I won't stop you."

"I'm not sure I'll have the luxury of quitting." Midnight sighed as Peter finally walked over to her, his expression grim. "I think I'm about to get fired."

"That's ridiculous," Tabitha growled, her eyes blazing.

"Tabitha," Peter said. "Would you mind if I have a private word with Midnight?"

"Actually—" Tabitha started to say, but Midnight shook her head.

"It's okay," she told her friend, and Tabitha stalked back to the mausoleum, her black skirts billowing out around her. Midnight almost smiled. Despite everything, Tabitha never lost sight of who she was. Unlike Midnight, who seemed to spend her entire life making one mistake after another. Well, no more. If ASP didn't like the fact that different parts of her life blurred together, then that was too bad.

She turned to Peter Gallagher and raised her chin. "I'm not going to say sorry."

"I should jolly well hope not," he agreed with a twinkle in his eye. "In fact, before you say anything at all, I want to congratulate you."

Wait. What?

Midnight wrinkled her nose. It had been a long day, and there was a good chance that her brain wasn't working properly.

"I did everything wrong, not to mention breaking a gazillion rules. I told Logan *and* Taylor. And you know what? The only thing I would've changed is that I didn't warn my sister sooner."

"Yes, I know." He nodded, his eyes still twinkling. Now she was downright confused.

"Why aren't you yelling at me?"

Peter led her over to where someone in his team had set up two chairs and a table. He ushered her to sit down and cleared his throat.

"Midnight, part of being a good field agent is learning discretion. When to follow the rules and when to break them. It takes most of our agents several years to understand what this really means. To weigh up the stakes and make big decisions."

Midnight opened her mouth and then shut it again. "So, I'm really not in trouble?"

"In trouble for stopping a person with the highest levels of planodiume that we've ever seen? For dealing with four planodiume ruptures? Not to mention managing to unbind the spectral energy that he'd been using? Midnight, trouble is the last thing you are. In fact, I'm happy to say that I'm promoting you."

"A promotion?" She widened her eyes.

"Does that mean better security clearance on the database?" Tabitha called out in a hopeful voice. Obviously her lip-reading skills were improving.

"It does. And another rulebook. Though actually, we shouldn't call it that. It's more of a skill book than anything. Teaching you how to deal with a whole range of dangers, some of which you've already experienced firsthand."

Midnight took the book, the leather smooth against her hands. She flipped it open to page one:

Forget everything you were told in the previous handbook...

"I think I could get used to this." Midnight grinned before something else occurred to her. "What will happen to Dylan?"

"We've administered the antidote to clear the planodiume from his system, though it will take awhile for that to work. And then he will have to undergo rehabilitation in Europe."

"I guess that means he'll be getting his gap year after all."

"I'm not sure it will be that enjoyable for him. Of course we will need to talk to his family. We're not in the habit of kidnapping people...unlike Dylan. But we'll also take steps to ensure he can never do something like this again," Peter said before frowning as his cell phone flashed. "I'm sorry. It looks like there's an emergency in Greenland. I'll have to take this."

"Of course." Midnight nodded as Taylor walked toward her. She was clutching a similar blanket, and her face was pale. Midnight had no idea what the ASP agents had said, but she imagined her sister probably had some questions.

"Well, I guess now you know. I really am a freak," Midnight said in a light voice, but instead of answering,

Taylor dragged her into a fierce hug. The tension in Midnight's chest loosened as they finally drew apart.

"Trust me, I've never been more pleased to see anyone. Freak or not," Taylor said as she sat down in the chair Peter Gallagher had vacated. She toyed with the edge of the blanket. "I still can't believe everything that happened today. And that my kid sister can see…spectron energy?"

"Spectral," Midnight corrected with a weak smile. "I'm so sorry I didn't tell you. I should've warned you how much danger you were in."

"According to Geoff—who, by the way, is supercute. Plus his English accent is hot—"

"Taylor." Midnight coughed.

"Right, so according to Geoff, even if you'd told me, I most likely wouldn't have believed you if I hadn't seen it with my own eyes. Not that I saw all of it. Just the last part. Geoff explained that sometimes when huge amounts of spectral energy are released, even nonsighted people can see it," Taylor said before breaking off. "Was it as scary as it sounded?"

Midnight pressed her lips together. She was about to lie and pretend it was fine, but lying was what had put her sister in so much danger. "Yeah, it was kind of terrifying."

"My kid sister. A superhero. Hey, is that why you were always out babysitting?"

Midnight nodded. "It was my cover."

"Nice," Taylor said as her cell phone beeped with another text message from their mom. Taylor studied the screen and then looked up. "They're going to be in Berry in an hour and want a full explanation."

Midnight nodded. As soon as ASP had arrived, Midnight had sent her mom a text message to say that Taylor had come home and was fine. It wasn't quite the truth, but she didn't want her mom to worry while she and Phil were on the road. However, when she was home…

"Don't worry. I'm going to tell them the truth. Peter Gallagher said I'm responsible enough to make my own decisions, and they deserve to know the truth."

"What? Are you out of your mind?" Taylor snapped, looking more like her usual self. "You can't tell them the truth."

"But I have to," Midnight protested. "You could've been killed. I'm not sure you understand just how dangerous Dylan was."

"Oh, I understand. Geoff explained everything to me. With diagrams. But that's not your fault. It's Dylan's. And if you tell Mom the truth, you'll never be able to leave the house again. I mean, can you imagine?"

"Considering how she reacted to the party you wanted to go to, you could be right," Midnight admitted.

"Of course I'm right," Taylor declared. "And now that I know how important your job is, I also know that you need to leave the house to do it. See where I'm going with this?"

Midnight blinked. Was this really her sister? They normally couldn't even agree on pizza toppings. And Taylor was forever teasing her about the smallest thing. And yet now Taylor was actually trying to help her?

"Okay, but if we don't tell her the truth, what *do* we tell her? I mean every other option will get you in trouble."

"I can handle that," Taylor said in a firm voice.

"You'd really do that?"

"Hey, you rescued me and never once said 'I told you so,'" Taylor said, her face softening.

"Taylor, it wasn't your fault.

"No, and it wasn't your fault either. So, stop blaming yourself. The fact you've been doing this for six months is kind of awesome."

"Thanks," Midnight said as an ASP agent came over with the instructions to drive them all home. Midnight got to her feet and smiled at her friends. It really had been some night.

CHAPTER TWENTY-FIVE

"And may Thor look down upon this handfasting and strike his hammer to those who may oppose it, bringing to them a painful and brutal death," the celebrant said as she wrapped the final piece of string around Midnight's mom's hand, connecting it once and for all to Phil's.

Her mom looked beautiful. Blond curls streamed down her back, all threaded with small beads, shells, and flowers. The blue dress she'd made brought out the sparkle in her blue eyes, while Phil looked handsome, dressed in full leather with smears of black on his cheeks.

On their fingers were matching silver rings carved with runes on the outside and with their initials engraved together on the inside. It was kind of cute.

Somewhere a raven cawed, and buttery sunshine shone down on the hillside. Daffodils and wildflowers poked out amid the sea of swaying green grass, just like her mom had imagined. Next to her, Taylor shifted, the fabric from her shield maiden costume brushing against Midnight's arm. Taylor's eyes glittered, almost as if she was about to cry, but she wiped them before Midnight could be sure.

After their mom and Phil kissed, they drank once more from the large horn and everyone in the wedding party started to cheer and stomp, because apparently that's what happened at Viking weddings.

"Wow," Malie said as she raced along the grass to where Midnight was standing. She was closely followed by Logan. Not far behind were Tabitha and Tyson Carl (who, if Midnight didn't know better, had been holding hands). "Viking weddings are the best. I wish I'd dressed up."

"You'll have to come along to the next party they have," Midnight said as she smoothed down her own dress. Since using Phil's armor had helped keep them safe two weeks ago, she now had a new appreciation for it.

"I'd love that," Malie said just as Tabitha and Tyson dragged her off to meet Ruth and Elsie, who'd both come along to the wedding looking resplendent in long, velvet gowns and with crowns of flowers in their hair. Which left just Midnight and Logan.

"Hey," he said, a tangle of dark hair falling across his face. "That was pretty cool. Your mom seemed happy."

Midnight looked over to where her mom and Phil were giggling like kids over something or other. The stress that had been following her mom around like a dark cloud had disappeared as soon as she'd arrived home and seen Taylor. Her mom had immediately hugged them both and declared that it didn't matter what the weather was like for her wedding. All that mattered was that the people she loved were safe.

Of course, thanks to the fact that Dylan was no longer wielding the Black Stream and going crazy with planodiume, the weather had instantly improved.

Something that wouldn't have happened if Logan hadn't stepped in.

"Thanks again for helping," Midnight said before shyly looking at him. "And for not thinking that I'm weird."

"Weird?" His cheeks brightened. "Midnight, you're the coolest girl I've ever met. Your stepdad's a Viking. Your mom has her own YouTube channel, and you see ghosts. I only wish I could be half as weird as you."

Her heart pounded as she began to smile. "You're pretty weird yourself. Who turns up to a Viking wedding with a deerstalker hat on?" she said, knowing that several of Phil's friends had already admired the fact it was an authentic one that Logan had saved for months to buy.

"I guess we make a good team," he said before giving her a shy smile. "Which is why I was wondering if you'd like to go on another date."

"Really?" Midnight's eyes widened. On their last date, she'd been so worried that she might slip up and say something she shouldn't. Or that he'd find out the truth about her and not like her anymore. But this time... "I'd like that. A lot."

"Great." He smiled as Tabitha came flying over to them. Her black Viking dress and armor clattering as she moved.

"I just had a message from Peter Gallagher," she announced, her cheeks glowing. "We have a new case."

"We?" Logan's eyes lit up as he looked from Tabitha to Midnight. "As in me too?"

"Well, yeah," Midnight said. "I mean, if you want to. Of course, now that you know how dangerous it can be, we would totally understand if you said no."

"Are you kidding?" Logan yelped. "That would be amazing. I'd love to."

"Yeah, well, the first thing you need to do is get that goofy look off your face," Tabitha deadpanned. "If you want to work with us, you need to take it seriously."

"Goofy?" Logan tried to protest. "This isn't goofy. It's just my regular face."

Midnight smiled at him as Tabitha held up her phone to show them the message. "It could be worse. Last week she was trying to convince me we should all wear capes."

"And I stand by that. Think how handy a cape would've been during all that rain," Tabitha retorted with a smile. "Now, do you want to hear about this new case or not?"

Acknowledgments

To the usual suspects, Sara Hantz and Christina Phillips. No books get written without you two by my side, and for that I'm grateful!

Thank-you to Susan Hawk for being such a fan of this series and for finding it such a great home! A big shout out to the amazing Eliza Swift, who is a story ninja in the very best sense of the word! And to Wendy McClure, Alexandra Messina-Schultheis, the amazing art department, and the entire team at Albert Whitman. Thank-you so much for all the hard work.

And finally to my mother, Pam Ashby, for helping me become a lifelong reader. There's really no better gift you could've given me.

CATHERINE HOLT was born in Australia but now lives in New Zealand, where she spends her time writing books and working in a library. She has a degree in English and journalism from the University of Queensland and is married with two children. She also writes books for older readers under the name Amanda Ashby and hopes that all this writing won't interfere with her Netflix schedule

100 Years of

Albert Whitman & Company

1919–2019

Albert Whitman & Company encompasses all ages and reading levels, including board books, picture books, early readers, chapter books, middle grade, and YA

Present

2017

The Boxcar Children celebrates its 75th anniversary and the second Boxcar Children movie, *Surprise Island*, is scheduled for 2018

The first Boxcar Children movie is released

2014

2008

John Quattrocchi and employee Pat McPartland buy Albert Whitman & Company, continuing the tradition of keeping it independently owned and operated

Losing Uncle Tim, a book about the AIDS crisis, wins the first-ever Lambda Literary Award in the Children's/YA category

1989

1970

The first Albert Whitman issues book, *How Do I Feel?* by Norma Simon, is published

Three states boycott the company after it publishes *Fun for Chris*, a book about integration

1956

1942

The Boxcar Children is published

Pecos Bill: The Greatest Cowboy of All Time wins a Newbery Honor Award

1938

1919

Albert Whitman & Company is started

Albert Whitman begins his career in publishing

Early 1900s

Celebrate with us in 2019!
Find out more at www.albertwhitman.com.